Riot

A riot in the lifers' wing of Brentford Prison results in the death of an IRA prisoner. Chief Superintendent Walsh and Detective-Inspector Roberts are immediately involved in the kind of horror case CID officers always try to dodge: beset by red tape, staff obstruction, the lies and deceit of the prison subculture. When prison staff are implicated, there is also pressure from unions, from Whitehall administrators; ultimately from politicians.

Walsh, nearing retirement, has no desire to crusade against the Law-and-Order Establishment. Yet there are limits to his readiness to compromise and play along with the System. Moreover, the detectives' dilemma is compounded by the resourcefulness of ITN crime reporter Kate Lewis, who, having cultivated a liaison with DI Roberts, learns of a top-level cover-up.

Walsh is soon made aware that his own retirement prospects are at risk; so too, though he does not know it, is Kate's life.

ROGER PARKES

Riot

With a Foreword by
Robert Kilroy-Silk, MP

Chairman, Parliamentary Penal Affairs Group

COLLINS, 8 GRAFTON STREET, LONDON W1

William Collins Sons & Co. Ltd
London · Glasgow · Sydney · Auckland
Toronto · Johannesburg

First published 1986
© Roger Parkes 1986
© in the Foreword, Robert Kilroy-Silk 1986

British Library Cataloguing in Publication Data

Parkes, Roger
  Riot.—(Crime Club)
  I. Title
  823'.914[F]   PR6066.A6953

  ISBN 0 00 231498 3

Photoset in Linotron Baskerville by
Rowland Phototypesetting Ltd
Bury St Edmunds, Suffolk
Printed in Great Britain by
William Collins Sons & Co. Ltd, Glasgow

FOREWORD

Riot is a thriller, and a very good one. But it is more than that. It is also a thoroughly-researched and well-informed indictment of our system of criminal justice and, more particularly, of our penal estate.

Our overcrowded and obsolescent prisons are in turmoil. Over a third of today's record population of 48,000 prisoners are compelled to share two or three to a cell built for one in Victorian times. They have no proper access to sanitary facilities, are denied adequate opportunities for work and recreation, and endure physical conditions that fail to meet the most elementary standards of human decency and violate internationally agreed standards for the treatment of prisoners.

Such circumstances create tensions and serious hardship for both prisoners and prison staff. Not surprisingly, therefore, there have recently been several riots in our prisons—of the kind accurately portrayed in *Riot*—culminating in serious injuries to inmates and officers.

The background to, the causes of, the action during, and the consequences after such 'disturbances', as the Home Office prefers to describe them, are all faithfully recorded in Roger Parkes's exciting but chillingly realistic story.

Riot is a dramatic story full of pace and suspense. It's fiction. But it is so true to life, so tellingly descriptive of the cloistered, secret and unnatural world that is a prison, and displays such a deep knowledge of it, that it could equally well be taken to be an impartial and dispassionate account of a real event.

I do not think that one can pay an author a better compliment than that.

Robert Kilroy-Silk, MP
Chairman,
Parliamentary Penal Affairs Group

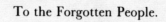

To the Forgotten People.

DAY ONE

CHAPTER 1

'Brentford—Take One.'

'News of the disturbance by inmates here at Brentford Prison followed on the sudden cancellation this morning of visits by inmates' families, probation officers and lawyers, all being refused entry and turned away. Meanwhile, since midday, there has been a hurried influx of extra personnel. So far a total of five busloads of prison officers has been rushed across from London's other main prisons—Pentonville, Brixton and Wormwood Scrubs—while here outside we've seen a burgeoning police presence, including units from the Special Patrol Group, among them several armed marksmen being . . . Damn that noise!'

Kate Lewis gestured skywards in frustration as the jumbo-jet thundered overhead on landing approach for Heathrow. For all her experience as a television reporter, she was still prone to camera nerves; so that, given a good start with no dries or line-fluffs, it was wildly exasperating to be drowned out by a jumbo . . . doubly so since they were ahead of the Beeb with the story and rushing to get a piece taped for the mid-afternoon news.

The story, although as yet light on details from inside, had all the makings: disruption within a high-security prison, good visuals of the extra staff being bussed in, deployment of the police SPG units and marksmen—exactly the boost Kate needed just now, always needed, come to that, given the dog-eat-dog nature of crime reporting.

'Where from?' she asked as the jet noise faded. 'Back to the top?'

'No, Kate, just pick it up on marksmen, and we'll cover

it with a cut-away to the police transits. All set then? Turn over. Brentford—Take Two.'

'. . . among them several armed marksmen being hastily deployed to vantage points around the outside of the prison. So far there has been no official word on the situation inside the prison itself, but ITN has learned that the trouble originated inside A Wing, the cell-block reserved for life-sentence prisoners. This is Kate Lewis of ITN outside Brentford Prison.'

Detective-Inspector Roberts, although he went along to the squad's viewing-room specially to watch the mid-afternoon newscast, did so with as yet little more than a spectator's interest. It had been a couple of hours earlier, at lunch in the canteen, that he and Spence had picked up the buzz from the ops room people about the SPG heavies being whistled off to Brentford nick, rifles and all.

'She's got to be right about the lifers' wing,' Spence remarked, switching off the set. 'They wouldn't be calling in the cavalry, *plus* shooters, just for a bit of hijinks in the YP wing. It's got to be something like the IRA.'

'Maybe.' Taff Roberts shook his head. 'Unless they're over-reacting, wanting to make it all a lot bigger than it is.'

'The screws inflating it, you mean?'

'Could be.' Taff shrugged, then asked: 'That Kate Lewis —you know her, don't you?'

'No such luck, mate. Harry Blake's the one who's in there.'

'Randy devil's married, isn't he?'

'Ah well, I'm not saying he's into a ding-dong with the lady. More of a *quid pro quo*, the way I heard it.'

'Hell of a risk with our press blokes just along the corridor. Mind, I reckon she'd be worth a few risks.'

'Fancy her, do you?'

'Hell, boyo, wouldn't you?'

What Taff Roberts would have fancied even more, however, was the chance to get out on a bloody good case, preferably a nice complicated homicide with plenty of over-time; anything rather than the dreary print-out comparisons he'd been stuck on for the last month or so. It was an occupational hazard, of course. Once an enthusiastic DI like him let the blessed job become a marriage substitute, a romantic blend of loyalty and ideals, then he was bound to be vulnerable when it was his turn for the desk chores—prey to lunch-time blues and fantasies about TV reporters.

A Wing's massed protest had in fact started as a compromise sit-in by the new Table Six men—the uneasy alliance of opportunists who had scrambled to fill the power vacuum left when the original Table Six men had been ghosted out to Wakefield and The Verne. Unsure of how much support they could muster and reluctant to go out on a limb with the Nigs and the Micks, they had started by limiting the protest to a sit-in.

Its success, drawing in well over 300 of the wing's 400 lifers, promptly reinforced their militancy. When the Nigs started to get a chant going, they gave the nod and joined in: *Rights, not favours . . . rights, rights, rights . . .*

Initial reaction from the wing staff had been low-key and cautious: Principal Officer Halldain had come out of the gate office and, watched by half-a-dozen officers, had come across to urge a bit of sense, lads. It was this that had triggered the chanting which had persisted in defiance of the repeated orders over the tannoy until late morning when the wing governor, Ashley Pelham, had finally come out to give them a hearing and then relay their grievances to the prison governor.

In the event, the governor left them to it for a further few hours before finally rejecting their demands—a delay which gave the militants the chance they needed to wind up the aggro to a pitch of intense bitterness. When, in mid-after-noon, Ashley Pelham came out to face them again, word of the rejection triggered an instant response. Anxieties which had festered during the long hours of waiting erupted into frenzied resentment. The wing governor and the discipline officers backing him up barely had time to fall back —half to the gate office, Pelham and the others to secure themselves in the wing admin office—before the mood of the hundreds of lifers hit flashpoint.

Kate Lewis and the rest of the ITN team heard the burst of noise erupt in A Wing. Then, like a flash-fire racing through undergrowth, they heard the roar of sympathy spread from one adjacent cell-block to the next—from the mid-termers doubled up in B Wing, to the remand men three to a cell in C Wing, to the young prisoners crowded together in D Wing—until there were few throats silent among the thousands of inmates . . . bellowing and swearing and clattering whatever metal objects they could find to whack against the window grids.

   To the roar from A Wing was soon added the crash of vandalism. The newspeople gathered outside could hear the wholesale splintering of wood, smashing of crockery and later the thud of masonry as fittings were wrenched from the ageing walls of the cell block. It was a sound—the combination of animal yells and concentrated destruction —somehow deeply atavistic, a savagery devoid of reason.

To life-sentence prisoner B48403 Ronald Arthur Hythe, the excitement was intense, surging wildly through his veins, heady and enthralling. Yet it was not total intoxication, not a consuming mania; after the first hysterical burst of violence, sanity returned enough for him to register the possible threat to young Butch, the over-sexed cock budgie with which he shared his cell.

   Since the main force of destruction was still centred down in the well of the block, Ron Hythe had little difficulty getting up to the Threes landing and reaching his cell, where he leaned back on the bed after freeing the little bird. He watched it fuss around the cell and then let it perch on his head while he attempted some Grendon Think in an effort to get himself calmed down.

Previously, before going for his year at the psychiatric prison, Ron Hythe had been existing rather than living: tense and depressed, shutting himself away in his cell all the time, consumed with a self-hate which extended to everything around him. With the year at Grendon, however, he had been born again, healing from morbid guilt to healthy remorse; rekindling a sense of self-esteem and, with it, the strength to purge the two sly voices of Phyllis and Sheila from his head . . . overall, indeed, a wondrous release from the prison of the mind.

Another aspect of Grendon liberation was his friendship with Tony Rogers. Before going to Grendon, Ron Hythe had scorned the slim, light-footed little bloke more sharply than just about any other of the lifers in A Wing. But now, since his year at the Funny Farm, Ron had found himself able to accept without fear or prejudice the advances Tony made to him—indeed, had welcomed their friendship as something beautiful and spiritual and, yes, miraculously loving.

Now, reclining in his cell, he went through the Grendon rituals—posture, rhythmic breathing, mantra—but all to little effect. What with the continuing racket and frenzy of destruction outside, the vibes were all wrong. He reached up and extricated Butch from his hair, kissed the stubby little beak, popped the bird back in its cage and then stepped outside on to the iron balcony of the Threes landing. He hesitated over pulling the massive steel door shut, thus locking out not only intruders but also himself. But then, glimpsing Tony down among the seething turmoil of inmates below, he slammed it shut and ran yelling along towards the stairs.

*

It was barely half an hour after the riot had flared into action that Kate Lewis detected a sinister change in the noise from A Wing: a shift from hooligan vandalism to physical aggression and battle. The tone of the inmates' voices surged to a pitch of angry retaliation and, simultaneously, the depersonalized cackle of a loud-hailer could be heard calling out tactical orders of attack as the anti-riot force went into action.

'Black section north to clear a way up to the Twos . . . Red section south to support Yellow . . . Green section rally and help clear the Twos . . . Regroup Yellows, regroup and support the Reds . . . Browns north and up to the Twos . . .'

And by then, gradually but steadily, the wild yells in retaliation had begun to give way to shouts of pain, fear and panic.

Coincident with all this came the undulating wail of sirens as first one and then a second ambulance roared along the main road and, headlights cutting through the afternoon drizzle, swung in between the gateposts where, after a brief pause for the boom to be raised and the main doors swung open, they were swallowed into the prison. Even as their sirens died away, so too did the remaining noise from inside the cell block. A couple more distant barks from the loud-hailer; and then nothing to hear other than the prevailing hum of Brentford High and the whine of the next jetliner on descent to Heathrow.

'Jack Walsh here.'

'The deputy commissioner would like a word in his office, please, sir. Priority.'

'Not my expenses again.'

'No, this is priority, Chief Superintendent.'

Jack Walsh was already reaching for his jacket as he rang off, straightening his tie, smoothing his hair—but out of respect for senior rank rather than for the man who held it. Look smart, quick off the mark: the outward manifestations

of discipline so essential in the service which was also
a force. Alertness, efficiency, accountability, adherence to
regulations, respect for rank—these were the criteria by
which Walsh had worked his way up to chief super—and
not now to be relegated just because retirement was in sight
and he was out of kilter with a certain whizzkid appointed
over him as deputy assistant commissioner.

'You wanted a word, sir?'

'Take a seat, Jack. Be with you directly.'

After all, DAC Crime was a front job: less in fact to do
with crime than with image and PR, with budgets and
admin; doubtless ideal for plummy-voiced college lads like
Frank Blaize but lost on a detective like Jack Walsh.

'I imagine you'll welcome a break from trade-union
fraud.'

'For a nice jolly out to the Cayman Islands—any time,
sir.'

'For heaven's sake, your expenses would bankrupt us.'
The DACC sat back, his smile unctuous. 'No, Jack, this is
a murder. I'd been hoping to find you one to go out on.'

'Most considerate, sir.' He knew there was bound to be
a catch in it somewhere with this young upstart. 'Whereabouts?'

'Brentford Prison. IRA bomber killed during the riot
there this afternoon.'

'Charming.' Walsh fumbled in his pocket, a reflex from
his smoking days. 'Ever done a job in prison, have you,
sir?'

'I haven't, no, but you have. Which is why I'm putting
you on this one. Experience, discretion, reliability, the authority of a seasoned DCS . . .'

'Good old Jack Muggins, eh.' He stood up. 'Who's with
me?'

'Bearing in mind your usual preference for a small team,
what about making a start with just DI Roberts?'

'Fine.' Walsh couldn't resist a grin. 'Young Taff won't

find himself much in the way of female interest in Brentford nick.'

'Just as well.' The DACC was still smiling as he waved him on his way. 'It's a delicate one, Jack. Keep me posted.'

Still Kate Lewis and the others waited. It was almost an hour now since the violent termination of the riot: the police marksmen all recalled from their vantage points and all but one of the SPG transit vans now departed; first one ambulance out and now the other. And still no statement. Numerous press reporters, news and camera teams all crowded along the railings and spilling back on to the road; yet from the massive Victorian-built prison across the forecourt, nothing but closed doors and silence . . . that compulsive secrecy and aversion to public scrutiny, that reflexive urge for concealment, that uneasy blend of paranoia, arrogance and indifference.

Not until 16.55, shortly before the evening shift change was about to release a flow of off-duty officers, did a spokesman at last emerge from the gate office. Even then he wasn't directly from the prison but a Home Office man, Philip Knowles, the regional director.

The ITN team had taped the arrival of Knowles's Whitehall car a couple of hours earlier. Now they taped the man himself as, holding an umbrella and escorted by a couple of officers, he moved forward to the vehicle boom. He gestured for the police to let the press crowd forward, then waited motionless and formal for the camera, lighting and sound to be set up. At last, passing his umbrella to one of the officers to hold over his head, he pulled out a written statement, copies of which were already being distributed to the press by the other officer.

'Ladies and gentlemen, protest in the form of a sit-in was commenced this morning by long-term prisoners in A Wing. The protest organizers presented numerous demands to the wing governor who relayed them to the governor of the prison, Mr William Hanford. The governor, after consultation with the Home Office, decided that, in the context of such protest action, these demands were totally unacceptable.

'Meanwhile, in accordance with security procedures established for such mass breaches of prison discipline, the governor had requested a police presence to ensure external security and also the assembly of a MUFTI squad trained in the Minimum Use of Force for Tactical Intervention. Once both these forces were safely deployed, the governor relayed his rejection of the demands to the protesters.

'Their immediate response was to resort to action of a violent and destructive nature. Fighting also broke out among the rioters themselves, to such a degree that eventually the governor, fearful of fatal injuries and also for the safety of the two dozen staff trapped inside the wing, ordered the Mufti squad to restore order. In the main, this was achieved with a minimum of injury to prison personnel and inmates alike.'

The Home Office man paused, glancing briefly up from the typed statement. Then, as the questions started, he held up a hand and resumed reading.

'It is to be expected that in due course an official inquiry will be ordered, as has been the case following previous such incidents at prison establishments elsewhere.' Pause. 'Furthermore, an independent police investigation has already been initiated into the death during the incident of one inmate whose name will be released as soon as his next of kin have been informed.'

Civil servant Knowles removed his spectacles and folded them away as, with an air of finality, he started to move back from the vehicle barrier.

'Thank you, ladies and gentlemen. I regret that it's impossible, for obvious reasons, to answer any individual questions. Copies of the statement are available to you. Since further information will be released *only* through the Prison

Department press officer, I respectfully suggest you should now disperse.'

'Ever done a nick job before?'

'No, guv'nor. The only times I've been inside were to interview villains.'

'You've got a few surprises coming, then.'

DI Roberts grunted, slowing the car as they reached the end of yet another traffic tailback. Then, after a quick check, he flicked the headlights to beam, switched on the blower and pulled out to race forward in face of oncoming vehicles. Walsh let him make some progress, then gestured him left into a clear space and switched off the blower.

'What's all the hurry?'

'A murder, guv'nor.'

'Which happened the better part of an hour ago. One thing you're due to find out is that about the *only* thing to get a shift on in prison is rumour. The rest is very, very turgid.'

Walsh paused, recalling with extreme distaste an investigation into the malicious wounding of a West Indian psychopath in the segregation unit at Wormwood Scrubs.

'Another thing you'll learn is that it's all very closed up.'

DI Roberts glanced sidelong at his chief. 'Goes without saying, surely.'

'It's not the doors I'm talking about, son, so much as the people.'

CHAPTER 2

The police allowed the ITN team back into the forecourt so that Kate Lewis could stand against the barrier with the stream of off-duty staff leaving from the gate-office door as backing to the take. In the event, there were no interruptions from jumbo jets this time, but instead DI Roberts swinging his Rover in from the main road and letting go with the blower to get the barrier raised.

Cameraman Peter Marse nipped smartly backwards so as to tape their arrival, tightening his shot on to Walsh as he held out warrant and ID cards, the sound man dipping a boom mike neatly across to catch the gate-officer's words as he radioed the details to the office.

'Detective Chief Superintendent Walsh, Detective-Inspector Roberts and two forensic men.'

Reporter Lewis, meanwhile, isolated on the further side of the car, found herself graced with a broad grin of apology from the DI.

'Sorry to barge in on you like that, Miss Lewis.'

He added a wink, jerking a thumb towards his chief, then reversed the car slightly so she could edge round the front. Kate waved in thanks. Then, timing her move to coordinate with that of the lighting man, she moved round to the open passenger window.

'We just heard about the fatality, sir. I understand you're here to start the investigation. Any comment for ITN?'

Briefly she glimpsed the man's face: eyes hard and penetrating beneath jutting eyebrows, lean cheeks creased in a sardonic grin above the obstinate set of his jaw. He offered no comment, merely reaching past her to retrieve the warrant cards and then immediately raising the window.

The massive oak doors of the gatehouse started to swing open at the same time as the vehicle boom was raised. But already, even as Taff Roberts started to ease the car forward, Kate Lewis was taping in the pay-off.

'Shortly after five, little more than an hour after the crushing of the riot, and already the CID team, led by veteran Scotland Yard detective, Chief Superintendent Walsh, is moving in to commence an investigation of the violence which left one prisoner dead and many more injured. Kate Lewis, ITN News, Brentford Prison.'

*

'Dog-faced media bitch.'

'Only doing her job, guv'nor.'

'Something to be said for these walls if they're going to keep her off our backs.'

Taff Roberts grunted, reluctant to yield to the old man on it. True, Walsh's disdain of the press was routine enough in coppers of his generation, men who had served their cadetships well before it became fashionable to revile the force as racist, corrupt and brutal; before the beat men mobilized into pandas and the Permissive Society inverted traditional attitudes.

Yet, even allowing for this and the rash of radical TV documentaries that had accompanied it, Walsh's aversion to the press struck his DI as excessive.

Besides, damn it, fantasy apart, Kate Lewis was certainly not dog-faced. Austere perhaps: that hairstyle, those heavy glasses, her formal style of dress. But most probably that was just part of the job image: part of ITN's assumption that their leading crime reporter should present as a sort of policewoman-cum-prosecutor. Taff Roberts always preferred to allow a woman, especially one as well put together as she was, the benefit of the doubt.

An officer waved them across to park near some Portakabins ranged beside the high steel wall of the inner security fence. The principle of the double ring for high-security prisons had followed from the Mountbatten report. The original outer perimeter of Victorian ramparts was now augmented by constant video-camera surveillance and also a modern inner security stockade of toughened steel plates, surmounted at a height of five metres with coils of barbed wire. Entry into this inner stockade was by a single, permanently-manned gateway. The area between the inner and outer security rings housed the prison admin offices, staff canteen, visiting hall and pre-release hostel, and was also the subject of frequent dog patrols.

'Chief Superintendent Walsh?' The officer gave a token

salute as the chief got out of the car. 'Principal Officer Blake, security. Governor sends his respects, sir. He can't get across to meet you himself, account of debriefing the wing staff. I understand the wing governor's on his way over instead.'

The officer glanced towards the inner perimeter gate, then cleared his throat in apology. 'He shouldn't be long, sir, if you and your team would care for a cup of coffee.'

'Rather get cracking, thank you, Mr Blake.'

'Right, sir.' The PO gestured them towards the gate, then radioed central control to unlock for them before resuming to Walsh: 'The deceased has been shifted across to the prison mortuary, sir, if you'd care to make a start there.'

The mortuary was small and tiled in green, the further end taken up with the double doors of the body storage chamber. In the centre, beneath a lamp cluster, was a dished metal trolley on which the bulging polythene body-bag had been laid out.

DI Roberts was just starting to remove the bag when a tall, bespectacled man hurried in to join them, his features drawn with fatigue.

'Sorry to miss you at the gate. Ashley Pelham, wing governor.' His wire-rimmed glasses and grey suit supported the impression of a vague, abstracted cleric. He moved across to rinse his hands in the adjacent sink, indicating the spattering of filth on his trousers. 'All messed up. Sorry. When we go across to the wing, you'll see why.'

Walsh nodded, then turned to the trolley as his DI slid the body-bag clear. The corpse was that of a sturdy, robust, barrel-chested man of about thirty-five. In life he must have had the red face of a countryman; in death the complexion had darkened to a blotchy puce. The head was lying over at an unnatural angle and, checking the articulation, Walsh found it loose and floppy, the neck clearly broken.

'These marks,' Pelham put in, indicating various areas of skin grazing and laceration. 'It's probable most of them happened after his death.'

'After? How do you mean?'

'I'm afraid there was somewhat of a misunderstanding.' He hesitated, glancing round to where the security officer was standing in the doorway. 'Thank you, Mr Blake, I'll see to the liaison detail now.' He waited until the officer had gone before resuming his explanation to Walsh. 'An over-zealous stretcher team, I'm afraid. Officers helping out. They said they thought he was just unconscious—like the other man, like Hythe . . . They only realized he was dead when he—er—slid off on the way down from the Fours.'

'God's sake . . .'

'Circumstances have been—er—far from normal in A Wing, as you'll see.'

'None the less, I'll want to question these two stretcher clowns.'

'I rather think they went off duty.'

'Tomorrow then, Mr Pelham.'

'Certainly.' He rubbed at his forehead, eyes blinking in renewed weariness. 'The two main witnesses—McGuire and Connolly—I put in cells near my office in A Wing.'

Walsh grunted, then took another look at the corpse before gesturing for the forensic photographer to get busy.

'Has anything been done about a pathologist?'

'I believe the MO said he'd see to that. They usually send someone over from the Hammersmith Hospital.'

'Right then, let's get over to A Wing and see where it happened.'

Reflections from the high arc lamps glistened up from the rain puddles outside. The place seemed oddly hushed as Pelham led them past the first two cell blocks and then along under the covered way flanking the chapel. Only when they turned along under the lee of A Wing itself was the silence broken by shouts from the inmates overlooking them —indistinct jeering and obscenities from throats already hoarse from hours of yelling.

The entrance to the lifers' wing was situated midway along the side of the block. Beside it a dog-handler watched in silence, his huge Alsatian motionless beside him.

'About facilities,' Walsh remarked as Pelham reached for his keys. 'We're going to need a secure incident room— suitable for interviewing, communications and so forth. Also a couple of beds in case we decide to stay overnight.'

Pelham nodded, unlocking the massive outer door. He ushered them through into the entrance alcove, then re-locked before turning to unlock the barred inner gate.

As they entered, the Yard men reacted in disgust, first at the reeking stench in the place and then, going forward, to the devastation littering the ground-floor area. A bomb blast could hardly have caused more havoc. Everything even remotely movable had been wrenched down and smashed: wall-lockers, railings, tables, beds, chairs, were all scattered in tangled debris. The floor itself was awash with a dark, sludgy fluid which was still being added to by water dripping steadily down from the smashed recess toilets on each of the landings above. The resulting stench of sewage was worsened by the acrid, smouldering fumes from bedding and debris flung out and ignited on the chainlink safety-netting strung across between the balconies of the first landing. There was access to the upper landings only at the north end of the block, the narrow iron stairways at the south end still barricaded from top to bottom with bed frames and lockers.

With many of the electricity fittings torn down, the power to the cell block was still out, the cavernous building lit to shadowy effect by auxiliary gas and battery lamps. Here and there, teams of men, some in fire-fighting garb, others in sou'westers and boots, were beginning the task of mucking out this human midden. The impression, with the surrealistic lighting, was of some grotesque theatre of the macabre.

'Bloody hell, guv'nor.'

Walsh grunted an incoherent reply. Over the years, he

had experienced all manner of nauseating variations on the human condition but this lot was an altogether new dimension.

'This incident room you want,' Pelham said. 'As you can see, everything's flooded out in here. No proper lighting. Even the heating's on the blink. I suggest we fit you up with an office suite in the admin wing.'

'Rather depends if it'll impede access to witnesses.'

'There's no reason why it should. We can always find you escort officers.'

'All right, then.' Walsh nodded acceptance. He had no desire to stay any longer than he had to in this dreadful place. 'Where did it happen?'

'A recess up on the Fours—the top landing.'

With which, hoisting up his trouser legs like a dad at the seaside, Pelham paddled across through the floor swill to usher them up the iron stairway at the north end of the block. Three flights of stairs later, they reached the Fours where two young officers eyed them from the remnants of the glass-walled landing office.

Pelham paused, pointing along to the furthest extreme of the landing. 'The recess up that end.'

They started along, their feet clanking on the cast-iron balcony, past rows of cell doors, all of them now locked to contain the men whose brief fling of rebellion had ended in pain and humiliation.

In the toilet recess near the office a couple of men in wet overalls were struggling to shut off the water still spurting from ruptured pipe joins. A landing officer watched them in silence; a big, heavy-set man with a surgical dressing on his right hand. Further along, three more officers were carrying a tea urn and a tray of buns from cell to cell.

As they reached the furthest end of the landing, they saw there was another toilet recess. An officer stepped from it as they approached, moving aside to shine his torch down at the floor. To Walsh's surprise, the crude outline of a body had been chalked out CID-style on the floor below a row of washbasins.

'They found Doyle laid about there, sir.'

'What's that other mark?'

'That's where they found his assailant.'

'Who?'

'Ron Hythe, sir. Now in the prison hospital.'

By six o'clock in the evening the number of newsmen outside the prison had dwindled sufficiently for the police to let them forward into the forecourt. Kate Lewis gave it another half-hour in the rain before contacting the editor. For once Lawrence Cawley was unstinting in praise of their coverage for the early evening news.

'Delicious timing with that copper—really pipped the Beeb.'

'Believe me, Lawrence, it's as much as we're likely to get. None of the officers coming off duty were from A Wing and anyway they'd been ordered to steer very clear of the press.'

'What about the riot officers they brought in from the Scrubs and Brixton and Pentonville?'

'All bussed out again.'

'The A Wing officers are going to have to go home eventually.'

'Except they'll probably bus them out as well. Secrecy is second nature to these people. Did you get any joy from the Home Office?'

'Only the name of the dead prisoner. Patrick William Doyle. Done for the 1979 IRA bombing in Liverpool.'

'Steve know anything about him?'

'He's checking with his contacts in Dublin and Belfast right now.'

'What about the Westminster end?'

'The Home Secretary's unavailable—also both Shadows.'

'I could try for something from NACRO or the Howard League.'

'All right then, Kate, all right. But leave the team there a bit longer just in case.'

The bar room of the prison officers' club was crowded and noisy. The majority of officers coming off duty had headed straight in for a jar and news of the riot. There were queues of men outside each of the phone booths waiting to ring and reassure their wives. Any officer who had been anywhere near A Wing during the trouble was having to repeat the details over and over. Already, as the pints flowed, so the myths and rumours were evolving.

Ned Ballard, turning from the bar with a tray of pints, bellowed for a gangway and eased through the crush towards the side room occupied by members of the Prison Officers Association branch executive. So far the only item disposed of with unanimity had been Ned Ballard's round of pints.

Their mood was not eased by the presence of a member of the POA's national executive. John Tanner, a renowned trouble-shooter, had been rushed over to Brentford from headquarters in Edmonton at the start of the sit-in. Although scrupulously courteous in manner, he was none the less an outsider privy to what the others would have preferred to deal with themselves at branch level.

'Okay then, so here's how we read it so far,' Tanner began, checking his notes. 'Sit-in commenced shortly before dispatch of work parties. Instigated by Table Six plus the Nigs and the Micks. Usual impossible demands presented to Mr Pelham who relayed them to Mr Hanford. Governor for once had the good sense to confer with us—with me and Gerry, that is—at an early stage.'

'Bit suspicious, is that.'

'Maybe. But the fact is, he did it.' He nodded. 'And we accepted the principle of no concessions under duress.'

'Exactly how Table Six knew it would be.'

'Sorry?'

'Tribal warfare, mate—that's what it's all about.'

'Listen, right now we're getting sorted on the *facts*, okay? Right, then, Mufti assembled and briefed. Five sections of eighteen officers. Your section, the Blacks, detailed to spearhead up the north stairway after decoy action south by the Reds and Yellows. Blacks to continue up the north with the objective of securing the Fours. Greens to cover them on the Threes, and Browns to cover for both on the Twos.'

'Er—excuse me, Mr Tanner, but I thought there was a ruling against using local officers in Mufti teams. Reprisals and all that.'

'Recommendation, friend, not a ruling.' Tanner's retort was curt and dismissive. 'In the circumstances—manpower availability, local familiarity—the governor felt obliged to disregard it.' He nodded. 'A view to which Gerry and me gave our support.'

'Oh aye? And what about the Go? Did the governor consult you on that, too? Before he sent them in?'

John Tanner paused for a pull of bitter then gave a half shrug. 'Sort of. You know what Hanford's like. We were both there in his office when he gave the Go. Come the inquiry, he'll say we could have stopped him if we'd wanted to.'

'Crafty bastard.'

'Sure.'

'But did you want to, Mr Tanner?'

'Would *you* have wanted to? We could hear all hell going on inside the wing. We knew they'd got most of the shift trapped in there. I don't know about you, Gerry, but I kept thinking to myself, why doesn't he bloody well send them in, what the hell's he waiting for?'

There was a pause, eyes turning to Gerry who nodded in gloomy agreement. Yet it was a delicate issue, one which they knew would likely be central to the ensuing inquiry. *Did you not, by omitting protest, condone the use of the Mufti force?*

'Whose round is it, then?'

'Forget it, Gerry. Later, okay. Anyway, they got the Go, they stormed in, they stuck to the plan, and apparently it went off just like in a training exercise.'

'Yeah? Except for sodding Doyle and the forty-odd cons in hospital?'

'Leave it out, eh.'

'It's a *fact*. The hospital unit looks like *Emergency Ward Ten*. And that's without the ten really smashed-up ones they took to the Hammersmith.'

'Self-inflicted, Ned. Every one of 'em. You got that? Every single one. Either nonces or grasses.'

'Who are you kidding?'

Although the challenge was voiced by Reggie Boothe, Tanner well knew he was by no means alone in his concern. Brentford's committee, typical of most branch executives, was as diverse in attitudes as the members it represented: some tough and intolerant, others caring and concerned, most somewhere in between. Damn it, given the stress of a job like theirs—controlling cons day in, day out, the bad, the mad and the sad, marshalling them, securing them, ensuring their welfare, conforming to regulations, sifting lies, rumours and slanders, responding to pleas for help and sympathy, riding out abuse and hatred and threats—such a job, in bleak, decaying prisons crammed to double their original capacity, was bound to bring out in some the best, in many the worst.

Tanner was acutely familiar with both extremes: with the 'wets' who still cared versus the 'brutes' pushed beyond caring. He also knew how, at Brentford Prison, the split between them usually stayed safely submerged under the skilled stewardship of branch secretary Gerry Dancer. One reason for Tanner's hurried presence that day, however, was because a full-scale riot was likely to force a crisis of conscience for the wets such as Ronald Boothe.

'Listen, Ronnie, we've got to be a hundred per cent solid

on this. Okay, so maybe some of the more lunatic cons ran on to a Mufti stave here and there. But for official purposes, there was no assault and no damage, wilful or excessive, caused by any officer. None.'

'Don't be ridiculous . . .'

'At worst,' Tanner persisted, 'at worst, the odd parrying blow struck in self-defence. Bound to be some retaliation, of course, what with half-a-dozen of our blokes injured and all. But that and no more, okay?'

The ensuing pause was awkward, spiced as it was with embarrassment. This time the eyes turned to Ned Ballard: jolly, jovial, contentious old bastard that he was. But for once Ned didn't argue the toss. He took a slow, deliberate pull of ale, his eyes going from one to the other over the rim of the tankard.

'Okay, Mr Tanner,' he said at last. 'Okay. And Pat Doyle? Same goes for him, too, does it? Self-inflicted?'

'Doyle was killed by Hythe.'

'That's just not *quite* how I heard it from one of the Greens.'

'That's the way it happened. Facts, Ned, not hearsay.' Tanner's voice was flat, his eyes lowered in evasion to the notes on his pad. 'Doyle was killed by Hythe in self-defence.'

Walsh leaned his elbows on the desk, wondering how much longer before Taff got back with the tea and they could get on with McGuire.

The office which had been cleared for them in the admin wing was austere but functional: a couple of plain wooden desks, four tubular-steel chairs, two old-dial phones, a lockable metal filing cabinet, a twin tape-deck brought in from the Yard and an adjoining room suitable for camp beds . . . sparse for an incident room, but then that was the way Walsh had come to prefer things with a contained case like this: simple and uncluttered, minimal manpower, himself upfront to ask the questions and gauge the answers . . . by far the best way, given that he was anyway going to be Jack the Lad, answerable for the outcome.

'You're sure of that, Mr McGuire? Self-defence?'

'Sure as I'm sat here with yourself and that recorder, aye.'

'The tapes aren't switched on yet.'

'Nor they are.'

Both turned as Taff Roberts came in sideways, edging the door open with care so as not to slop the tea mugs on the tray.

'Put them over there to cool off, please, Inspector. We wouldn't want Mr McGuire to suffer in any way while he's in our custody.'

There had been a long hold-up about security earlier on. After marching McGuire across to the admin block from A Wing, the escort officer had brought him into the incident room and then promptly moved across to sit on a chair in the corner. Asked to leave, the officer had insisted that was impossible. Escort duty regulations were absolutely clear that at no time must a Category A high-risk prisoner outside the inner security ring be left unattended by the officer in charge of him.

Walsh had groaned. Having in fact interviewed all the witnesses in the Wormwood Scrubs investigation inside *both* security rings, this was an altogether new problem to him. He had promptly dialled through to the wing governor.

'Mr Pelham, Mr McGuire does not want an officer present and nor do I. The windows of this office are all barred, as you know. Will you kindly authorize your officer to remove his security presence to the passage outside the door?'

Conceivably this solution would have been adequate at the Scrubs but not so at HM Prison Brentford. Here, as now emerged, no officer accepted such an initiative without first getting it cleared by the POA branch secretary. John Tanner's immediate ruling now was that no such authority was acceptable merely on the verbal say-so of a wing gover-

nor. The established Home Office principle for such interviews was that the security officer must remain at all times
in sight but out of hearing. Acknowledging that their office was
too small for this, Tanner insisted that any variant of the
regulations would require a written dispensation under the
signature of the prison governor, copies both on file and also
to the POA, di-da-d-i-da, di-da-di-da . . .

Fortunately, what with the riot, both the governor and
also the governor's secretary were still present at the prison,
the necessary paperwork was hence forthcoming with a
delay of only twenty more minutes . . . so that finally,
expressionless to the last, the escort officer had agreed to
remove both himself and the chair to the passageway outside
the office.

'While you were off getting us the tea, Mr Roberts, the
prisoner was saying how it looked to him like a chance blow
struck in self-defence by the other prisoner, Ronald Hythe.'

'That's it, chief. You ask Dom. He'll tell you the same.'

'That's your mate Dominic Connolly?'

'Dom and me were both up there in the recess with Pat
Doyle when . . .' He checked, pointing to the tape-deck.
'Suppose we have those tapes running now, chief. Make it
official, like. I know you haven't cautioned me and all that,
but if I'm to be blabbing on with no lawyer or officer present,
the least we can do is record what I'm telling you.'

'As you wish.' Walsh started the tapes, recorded the
identity and time and then nodded for McGuire to get on
with it. 'In your own words then, from the beginning.'

'Like I said, we was up there together in the recess on the
Fours. Me and Dom and Pat.'

'For how long?'

'Soon as we could get ourselves up there after the screws
stormed the wing. Should have been McGinty and Donahue
and the other politicos up there with us, but they got cut
off.'

'So this was part of a pre-arranged plan?'

'Survival plan, aye. All ten of us to pack in there together. United front, know what I mean.'

'No. What were you expecting to happen?'

'Victimization, of course.' He guffawed, the sound harsh and bitter in his throat. 'They don't call us the Irish Mafia for nothing.'

'You were expecting some form of assault in reprisal for the rioting?'

'Too bloody right we were. We got it and all! McGinty, Lacey and the others—that's not by chance they're stretcher cases right now. Would have been Dom and me laid out along with 'em if poor Pat hadn't been stretched out dead with us in the recess.'

McGuire paused, indicating the tea. Walsh switched off the tapes and nodded for his DI to pass one of the mugs across. The Irishman drank greedily, grimacing as the hot fluid stung his bruised lips.

'Something wrong?'

'No bloody sugar.'

'Sugar's bad for you, Mr McGuire. Makes for aggression. You're best having a smoke instead.' He nodded for Roberts to give him a cigarette, then restarted the tapes. 'All right, so when the Mufti force stormed into the wing, the three of you retreated as planned to the north recess up the top landing.'

'That's it, aye. Mind, it was a fair old shambles getting up there. The lads had blocked the stairways, see—barricaded them with beds and that for when the attack came. So of course everyone's having to clamber over all the stuff to get up there away from the screws. By the time we three had made it up to the recess, the screws had already cleared the first stairs and were fighting their way up to the Threes. Because of that, there was a load of burkes come panicking up after us, looking for somewhere to hide themselves, and a fair bunch of 'em heading for our recess. Naturally, since

we're expecting our mates along, we had to send 'em packing. Most run off along to the next recess—all except for
that maniac Hythe who seemed to think as how this mate
of his was hid in one of the bogs behind us. God knows for
why he thought that, because there was no one there. But
anyway, he kept yelling Tony, Tony, and trying to push in.
Well then, Pat Doyle—see, if you'd known Pat, you'd cop
how it was. Donegal man, see, farming stock, bit of a bruiser.
Anyroad, he was in a right lather was Pat. He gave a wild
yell and then piled into this nutter Hythe.'

He paused, signalling towards the tape-deck as he reached
again for the mug of tea. Walsh stopped the tapes but
kept his finger on the start button, waiting in silence until
McGuire had managed to gulp the rest of the tea into his
battered mouth.

'I—er—to be honest, I can't say I actually *saw* the fatal
blow. I seem to recall that Dom yelled to me. And when I
turned, there was Pat stretched out under the basins with
Hythe on top of him and Dom trying to pull him off.
Naturally I waded in as well. Hythe's head must have
clobbered into one of the basins as we pulled him off because
he went limp. Okay, so then Dom gets at it, trying the
mouth-to-mouth with poor old Pat. But no good. Neck
broken. Gone. Another dead hero. Another martyr to the
evils of British rule in Ireland. And—and God rest him.'

He paused, a hand rising in hurried piety to the tiny
crucifix on the chain around his neck as the other hand
made the four points of the cross.

'And then?'

'The screws came busting in, that's what. Helmets on,
visors down, batons swinging. By the grace of God, the lead
one must have sensed how it was—read the presence of
death or whatever—else me and Dom, we'd have copped
our beating, same as the others did.'

'Who was he, this officer?'

'How should I know that, chief?' The retort came too

fast, the reiteration too emphatic. 'No idea whatsoever. The visor down over his face, like I just said. Crash helmet over the rest; protective overalls like the others. No way of placing him. None at all.'

'The visor's only perspex.'

'Aye, but curved. Throws off the light from the face behind . . . what little light there was up there. Don't forget, the electrics was off and precious few windows in that damned hole.'

He paused, staring from one policeman to the other and then down at his hands which were locked almost as though in prayer.

'Anyroad, chief, what's it matter who he was? Poor old Pat was off with his Maker by then—clobbered down by a freak of chance in his tussle with that madman Hythe.'

During the interview, Roberts had been glancing through the Prison Department case file on Doyle. Once McGuire had been escorted away and they were alone, he slid it across to his chief.

'They suspected Doyle of extensive drug baroning—the hard stuff—but never managed to nail him at it. They did get him for all sorts of other mischief, however. In and out of the segregation block every few months.'

'What sort of mischief?'

'Violence towards other prisoners, insubordination, possession of just about everything illicit. However, his section officer's report credits him with being the number one in the IRA squad. Apparently he was known around the wing variously as General Doyle, Big Spud and Chief Mick. He drew what they call here an R-F 20—presumably a recommendation from the judge for a fixed 20-year life sentence—on conviction for the Liverpool bombing in 1979. But there's also a code reference here to a security file.'

'Army or Special Branch?'

Taff Roberts grimaced, leaning across to tap the relevant

section of the file. 'So secret they don't even tell us.'

'That'll be the army, then. Which means they'll resist showing it to us.'

He picked up the telephone and dialled the switchboard, duly hanging on for almost a minute before getting an answer. 'Operator, I want this phone permanently plugged through on an open line.'

'Sorry, sir. Security regulations. If you want the bar lifted, you'll need a written authority from the governor.'

CHAPTER 3

Kate Lewis decided against contacting either NACRO or the Howard League. Neither body could be expected to do more than trot out their usual line about the woeful inhumanity and ineptitude of the prison system, its gross economic lunacy in terms both of cash and human resources, the rigidity of government policy, of entrenched Home Office bureaucracy and so forth. Not that Kate disagreed with them. To her, the only rational use of prison was as a place for the secure containment of persistently violent offenders. But no way was any political party ever going to get itself voted into power on a policy of prison abolition or even reform. In terms of votes, prisons had always been a non-issue and would continue so; the system was an established reality, impervious alike to criticism and change.

Kate was well aware that none of this diminished the impact of the Brentford riot as a news story. Indeed, it was the hottest development in a month otherwise drearily overburdened with industrial news: a story not only appealing to the viewers' baser, more punitive impulses, but one exquisitely enhanced by the death of an IRA bomber, the ideal victim to sacrifice on the altar of the public's blood lust.

Kate was a dedicated professional who had worked her way up the ladder from provincial weekly paper to national daily, from general reporting to the City pages, thence to more overt crimes, and finally from newsprint to screen. As a professional, she had few scruples about feeding the public what they wanted, irrespective of how distasteful. The piper, after all, calls the tune.

So instead of NACRO or the League, she searched out library footage on previous prison riots, including her Penal Dustbin interview recorded with an erstwhile governor of Wormwood Scrubs who had warned of the explosive over-crowding and understaffing in Britain's prisons. Good angry stuff. Suitably edited down, it would be ideal background on today's riot . . . or so Kate had thought until, checking with the Home Office, she got through to Philip Knowles.

'You ought to remember that the riot occurred in A Wing which happens to have Brentford's *lowest* density of prisoners. One man to a cell, and a lot more privileged than inmates in the other cell blocks. Free association, cooking facilities, TV and so on until eight o'clock every evening; use of the recreation hall beside the wing. By some standards you could say a very pampered wing—although I dare say they'll have to forfeit a lot of those privileges as from today. In any event, Miss Lewis, far less crowded and—er—explosive than elsewhere.'

'Oh.' Kate was drawing angry red triangles on her note-pad. 'Then why did they . . .'

'Obviously I can't spell out any of the demands they were making—not at this stage. But let me remind you that A Wing is for life-sentence prisoners. Maximum-termers. The majority of them Category A, high-risk men. Hence what one might call our *bromide policy* of allowing them individual cells and extra privileges. A paradox, if you like, that the worst offenders should enjoy the most comfortable circum-stances. But at the same time, since they're faced with sentences of life imprisonment, they're bound to be potentially the most disruptive—as indeed they've just shown today.'

'Yes.' Kate placed a large red question mark in the top triangle. 'Not only disruptive but also thought to be in possession of firearms, hm?'

'I beg your pardon?'

'The governor had got police marksmen deployed around the prison. He'd hardly have done that with a view to gunning down unarmed convicts as and when they burst out of the prison.'

'Indeed not.'

To Kate's regret, she could detect no shift in the suaveness of the civil servant's tone.

'So were the inmates armed? Or even thought to be?'

'Miss Lewis, no official comment here. All right? However, if you're speculating about the presence of those marksmen, it could be you've got them aiming in the wrong direction.'

'Oh?' She added more red question marks as: 'You mean —er—some sort of external support was expected for the rioters?'

'You'll doubtless be aware, Miss Lewis, that there's a fair number of IRA prisoners inside Brentford's A Wing.'

'Anything to add to the broken neck, Doc?'

The pathologist swung round from the corpse to peer uncertainly at the two CID men in the doorway of the tiny mortuary. He rubbed his forearm across to wipe the sweat from below the band of his green skullcap, then tugged his face-mask down to liberate a grin of recognition.

'Jack Walsh. That old whore in Richmond weir, yes?'

'That's the one.' The two exchanged rueful grimaces in recollection. 'Taff Roberts, Dr Craig.'

The pathologist waved a heavily smeared surgical glove at the DI in greeting and turned to indicate the remains of Patrick Doyle.

'Considerably less poking about to do on this joker. As you say, broken neck. Caused by a neat blow to the vulnerable point just below the earlobe here.'

'Any ideas on the instrument of death?'

'None as yet. Could have been a karate chop with the side of the hand; could have been a blunt instrument such as, say, a table-leg or an officer's riot stick. I'll be checking for fibres at the point of impact, of course, but don't be too hopeful.'

He raised one of the dead hands, turning it over to display marks on the knuckles. 'From these contusions and also these bruises on the body, he'd evidently been in a bit of a scrap before the death blow. Also there's all this grazing and laceration which happened afterwards.'

'The wing governor said they let him fall off the stretcher on the way down the stairway.'

'Good God.'

'Apparently the two officers responsible are off home now. It's unlikely we'll get around to hearing any details from them until tomorrow.'

'A cast-iron stairway, I imagine. Worn bare of paint.' The pathologist shrugged, leaning over to check the grazing with a magnifying-glass, then shook his head in doubt. 'I'll double check; but again, it's unlikely I'll find anything to confirm that.' He straightened up, gesturing in apology. 'Sorry, Jack, not offering you much in the way of help with this one.'

'After all the effort you put into that rotting mess out of the river, I'll forgive you.' Walsh moved back to the doorway. 'We're just off upstairs to see suspect number one.'

'Might be useful to establish whether he's a karate practitioner.'

'With any luck, he'll admit to the whole thing.'

But Ron Hythe was not reckoning to admit to anything. For, concussion and sedation apart, he was in a blind panic and wished to God they'd just leave him alone with his throbbing head.

'Mr Hythe, you're not yet under caution. Nothing formal. Just a few preliminary questions. I take it you are aware of the circumstances: that officers found you unconscious in the recess up on the Fours landing near the body of another prisoner; moreover, that there were two other prisoners present, both of whom are alleging that you were in a fight with the deceased—a fight which they claim culminated in his death.'

Walsh paused, hoping for some response but equally well aware that truth and frankness are not generally valid currency in prison. He also knew that, for those convicted of more barbarous crimes, pretence was often the more preferable option: the usual phrase *the prisoner is coming to terms with his offence* seldom meant that he was now able to confront the naked facts of his brutality but rather that time and the system had helped him to apply the cosmetic necessary to make it acceptable both to others and to himself: he was stone drunk; he totally blacked out; he was obeying the voices; it was someone else . . .

'Mr Hythe, I'm CID, not prison staff. I'm not here to inquire about the riot in A Wing today, merely to investigate the death of the man you're alleged to have been scrapping with.'

Pause. 'Okay then, you remember the riot? Pretty rough when the officers all came storming in, yes?' Pause. 'You remember that? What did you do? No recollection? You were found up on the top landing, so evidently that's where you headed, hm?'

Pause. 'Looking for Tony, perhaps?'

'What?'

'Ah, you haven't lost the power of speech, then.'

'Tony all right, is he?'

'Tell you what, Mr Hythe, I could find out. Appreciate that, would you?'

The prisoner eyed him in hostile silence a moment, then grimaced in acceptance: trust the copper to nose out his vulnerable area.

DI Roberts, squeezed into the corner of the cramped hospital cell, was watching the contest with relish. True, given Walsh's experience as an interrogator, there could be little doubt of the outcome. Yet there was a style about it which deeply impressed Taff Roberts. The old man could be demanding and cantankerous and overbearing, inclined to pull rank and assume extremes of loyalty; there were DIs who grumbled that to be teamed with Walsh was to be relegated to the role of teaboy; yet for Taff there was the compensation of being schooled in the traditions of a master who was already something of a legend.

'Okay then, copper, so what are they saying?' Then, at Walsh's glance: 'Those lying Irish pigs.'

'Remember them now, can you?'

'Too bloody right! That prick McGuire, for one. And Big Spud Doyle. He's the one who shoved me.' He paused at a sudden thought, eyeing Walsh from beneath the surgical dressing. 'Here, you say one of 'em died. Not Doyle, by any chance?'

'That's right.'

'*Lovely*. Worst of a rotten bunch, he was. How'd he go? Screws kick his head in, did they?'

'A broken neck, Mr Hythe—allegedly broken by you.'

'Ah.' The eyes hunted away in renewed evasion. 'That bastard McGuire'd say anything.' Pause. 'He didn't mention the screw, then?'

'Screw?'

Hythe gestured almost casually towards the dressing on his head. 'The officer who walloped this lot on me.'

*

PRISON DEPARTMENT CASE FILE

HYTHE, Ronald Arthur, B–84043; D.O.B. 14.4.39

Sentence: Life (no R–F)

Security Rating: Category A

Conviction: Reading Crown Court, 10.8.82, for murder of Mary Anne Hythe (wife) on 12.10.81. Appealed against conviction, 8.3.83, pleading to manslaughter on grounds of diminished responsibility through temporary insanity. (Psychiatric reports available.) Appeal rejected 10.3.83.

Movements: Remanded HMP Brixton 12.10.81 to 10.8.82; dispersal assessment HMP Brentford 10.8.82 to 19.4.83; temporary transfer to HMP Grendon 19.4.83 to 27.2.84; returned HMP Brentford 27.2.84.

ANNUAL REVIEW BOARD: (20.9.84.) *Section Officer*: conduct quiet and polite; progress good despite D/R Tony Rogers.

Welfare Officer: Contact with parents resumed while at Grendon and now sustained via exchange of letters. Commenced visits from PV in April '84. Sat O-Level English and Maths this summer, obtained mediocre grades.

Board Assessment and Recommendation: Despite brutality of crime, Hythe's recent progress and conduct should merit recategorizing to B by end of year. This will then enable his eventual dispersal either to Blunderston or Maidstone.

'What does the section officer mean by "despite D/R Tony Rogers"?'

Walsh glanced up, the telephone pressed to his ear, waiting, waiting . . . 'Shorthand for Deviant Relationship, boyo. Totally alien to a hot-blooded Welshman like you. But then again, given several years banged up in the nick, even you might start to deviate.'

The chief turned, speaking into the telephone as it was answered. 'Hello, Heather. Is Mum there?'

'No.'

No. Just that. Why did it never occur to the young to

communicate? To say why, where, for how long, instead of always having to be asked? Probably choked off because it's her old dad calling and not her latest prat of a boyfriend— not Billy or Geraldo but just the stupid old buffer who pays the stupid old bills.

'Listen, Heather love, I'm out on a case.'

'That dumb union thing?'

'No.' Amazing that she'd registered the union case. 'This one's a murder.'

'Hey! Get you.'

'Yeah, big deal. Now listen, Taff and me are stuck here on it.'

'Where's here?'

So many questions! 'Never you mind. Just tell Mum I won't be back, okay? Tell her I'll try and call again but it may not be until the morning.'

'You wicked old villain. Staying out all night, not telling where.'

'All right, so I'm in the nick.'

'What?'

'Brentford Prison.'

'Hey, you mean that IRA bloke who got killed in the riot?'

'That's the one. Now just look after your mum for us, there's a good girl. Stay in for once. Do some studying or ironing or something. I'll call her tomorrow. Or else she can get me on extension 308. Write it down now: 308. 'Bye then, Heather.'

'Bye, Dad. Oh, hey, give my love to Taff, okay?'

'No!'

'*Dad . . .*'

'He deserves better.'

Walsh rang off, grimacing across at the young DI but unable to check a grin of sheer pleasure over their exchange.

'Feeling a little brighter now, Mr Hythe?'

'You're kidding. Bugger almost split my roof for me.'

'Yes, well, this is Dr Craig—police surgeon. He's going to take a look at the injury.'

'Why?'

'Because you're saying it happened one way whereas there could be other blokes saying it happened differently. Dr Craig might just possibly be able to tell us something one way or the other by looking at the actual injury. Now just sit up so he can get at that dressing.'

'Where's the point, guv? I'm going to get done for it anyway.'

'Not if there's evidence to clear you.'

'Yeah? You're never going to nail that screw with it. That's not the way things work. That's not the *system*—not in here it ain't.'

'Mr Hythe, I'm simply trying to get at the facts.'

'You trying to tell me you're on my side? Trying to tell me you *care*? Just a murderer, ain't I? Just another lifer. Just rubbish to you—one of the Forgotten People.'

'I'm on no one's side, Mr Hythe. All I care about is getting at the facts. Now are you going to sit up or not?'

Ronald Hythe gave a final, long-suffering sigh and then, grimacing at his stupidity, levered himself forward from the pillows and submitted to torture.

'You seen Tony yet?'

'No, but the nursing officer told me he's not among the injured.' Pause. 'I'll see him in the morning.'

'That's why I was up there, you see: looking for Tony.'

'Was that where you used to meet? The recess?'

'His cell's just along from there, up on the Fours. I'd checked for him there but no luck. Well, that was bad. That worried me. So then I thought maybe he'd be along at the —*ugh!* Watch it, Doc.'

'Sorry. Do you have any other injuries?'

'Not ones you could reach. Anyway, guv, that's how it was: I reckoned Tony'd be along at the recess, but then, when I went to try and look, there's these IRA gits in there.

Wouldn't even let me in to look—kept pushing me about. Then that turd Doyle took a great shove at me. I went spinning back, and then, right out of nowhere, there's this screw coming at me along the landing—stick up in the air like a bloody Samurai and—and *whack* . . .'

Philip Knowles wrapped his remaining chicken-and-cucumber sandwich away and slid it into a desk drawer before flicking the crumbs neatly from his blotter and crossing the office to usher the director general in from the hallway.

'Precious few developments, sir. As it happens, you could have stayed for the next act.'

'As it happens, Philip, I welcomed the excuse not to. Wagner and I really aren't compatible.'

Roy Grantley shrugged out of his coat, allowing Knowles to hang it for him while he moved to perch on a chair beside the desk. He sat erect, elbows on the arm-rests, hands joined, knuckles supporting his chin, eyes bright and alert. He's on a high, Knowles thought, really enjoying the situation: a small man who thrives on challenge and who is even capable of manufacturing trouble just for the hell of it. It was a vice which, while unusual, was by no means unique among the senior mandarins of Whitehall; tiresome to put up with, but preferable perhaps to complacency.

'How did you manage with William Hanford?'

'Strained civility might best sum it up.'

'Yes, he's a bit of an old diehard.'

Knowles frowned, turning away to pour them a brace of sherries. He had found himself wondering during the heat of the riot crisis that afternoon just how such an insensitive oaf had ever been appointed as governor—and to run a prison, moreover, which was not only one of the biggest high-security establishments in the country but with the most militant branch of the Prison Officers' Association.

'Did he have POA support for the Mufti assault?'

'Tacit, yes.' Knowles set the drinks carefully on the desk. 'Less so from the wing governor, Pelham.'

'Ah.' Grantley's knuckles jerked briefly to and fro beneath his stubbled chin. 'Well, the POA's the more crucial. What about the fatality?'

'Apparently—' Knowles paused to sip his sherry—'apparently it was straightforward self-defence.'

'By the prisoner—this man Hythe?'

'Apparently.'

'Category A?'

'Yes.'

'Psychopath?'

'Apparently not.'

'Pity.'

'Schizophrenic, though. Did a year at Grendon. Serving life on a rather nasty domestic murder.'

'I see. Open-and-shut, then?' There was a hint of wistful regret in his tone. But the knuckles were grinding again under his chin: as close, Knowles thought, as the DG was likely to come to yielding any comment. 'Do you know anything about the policeman?'

'Chief Superintendent Walsh? I'll check around.' Knowles reached for a pad to make a note for the morning. Given Grantley's links with the Deputy Assistant Commissioner at the Yard, it seemed odd that it should be necessary. Perhaps it wasn't.

'Cabinet meeting called for midday tomorrow. Home Secretary will want briefing beforehand.'

'Right, sir. But I doubt we'll get more than a preliminary report from Hanford before the end of the week.'

'Very well. But make good and sure Hanford's prepared to stand by it. The same goes for the copper.'

'Er—hardly be proper for me to liaise directly with him, sir.'

'All right then, leave that side to me. I'll have a word with the chief. Now, what about the media?'

'Painless enough so far, sir. If you're sure about the Wagner, you can hang on and see what line Kate Lewis is taking on *News at Ten*.' Knowles moved to top up their glasses. 'Penal dustbins and IRA snipers, I expect.'

Dominic Connolly was scared: deeply and genuinely frightened. DCS Walsh believed that, in common with horses, sharks, teachers and customs officers, detectives should be able to sense fear. He had learnt to read the aura of dread as clearly as that of deceit or of hatred. It was a language not necessarily of much help to him in terms of court conviction rates; indeed it could often serve merely to confuse and perplex rather than incriminate. Yet it was a language, none the less, in an arena of communication. And in Dom Connolly's case it spoke with vibrant clarity.

He sat bolt upright in front of the two detectives, a small man with bat ears and large brown eyes. Unlike McGuire, he made no request for tea or tape-recordings or cigarettes. He appeared to be a person of few opinions and less self-esteem. His case file told them he had now spent nearly seven years inside from the time of his arrest in Liverpool with Patrick Doyle, and was listed for transfer to Wakefield or Maidstone. Like Doyle's, his life sentence carried a judge's R–F recommendation that he serve at least twenty years. Unlike Doyle, he had managed to steer clear of trouble during his years in Brentford.

'What are you scared of, Mr Connolly?'

'Nothing.'

'Right then, let's try it again: you were up in the recess with Doyle and McGuire, and trying to preserve it as a refuge for yourselves and the other IRA inmates.'

'They never made it.'

'But you were expecting them.'

'So Pat Doyle reckoned. He said they were coming. But they never showed.'

'Who did come?'

'None of 'em. Just Pat and Kevin and me. Sure, there was one or two tried pushing in, but we kept 'em out.'

'Who? Can you name any of them?'

'Only that bloke Hythe. Only him.'

'What did he do?'

'Come raging in yelling for his poofter friend Tony.'

'What did you do?'

'Tried to push him away like the others.'

'You yourself?'

'No, it was Pat Doyle lit into him, not me.' He paused, face lowered, the fear surging in him like a spasm of cramp.

'Go on, Mr Connolly.'

'Can't rightly recall.'

'Try.'

'It was just a blur. Them two scuffling, like. Hitting out. Then suddenly Pat goes down—plonk—like he was pole-axed.'

'And then?'

'Hythe's down with him.'

He paused, glancing briefly up, first at Walsh, then at Roberts, and then down again.

'The two of 'em scrapping for their lives and then, next second, the two of 'em laid out flat on the recess floor. Hythe out cold and Pat Doyle with his neck broke.'

'Did you at any stage try to intervene?'

'No.' He shook his head. 'All happened too sudden for that.'

'Did Kevin McGuire try to intervene?'

'Not that I saw.'

'His story is different from yours on that, Mr Connolly.'

'Oh aye? Maybe he did, then.'

'What he told us was that *you* intervened.'

'What?'

'That you piled in to try and help Doyle.'

'Don't try getting clever with me now, copper. Don't think you can kid me along like that.'

'I'm not. Listen, we can play you the recording—you can

hear exactly what McGuire said. Mr Roberts, run the tape through to that particular part.'

'Well, he—er—bloody Kevin's mistaken about that.'

'Oh? He was very clear about it with us. He said how Doyle went down with Hythe on top of him.'

'Not as I recall it.'

'And that you jumped in to try and pull Hythe off.'

'No.'

'Then McGuire joined in to help you.'

'No.'

'And it was in pulling Hythe off Doyle that Hythe's head hit the washbasin and he was knocked unconscious.'

'*No.*' Pause. 'It was like I just said. All very sudden. The two of 'em scrapping one second and then both down and out on the floor.'

'What about the officer?'

Fear jerked again at the Irishman like an electric charge. 'Kevin say something about an officer, did he?'

'We're asking you, Mr Connolly.'

Pause. 'He—er—this officer, he came charging in while Kevin and me was looking at Pat Doyle.' Pause. 'Well, we both yelled at him how Pat was croaked.'

'What did he do?'

'Took a quick look and—and then he went off to help his mates in the fighting further along the Fours.'

'Could you identify this man? This officer?'

'No.' Pause. 'Too dark. Face hidden. No.'

'You have no need to fear reprisals, you know.'

'No.'

'Do you think Ron Hythe meant to kill Pat Doyle?'

'Meant to? No, I don't.'

'Just a chance blow in a scrap, was that it?'

'Aye. Pat went for him and he was fighting back. Just rough luck that old Pat bought it the way he did.'

'So you don't think, Mr Connolly, that it could have been deliberate?'

'You what?'

'That Hythe might, for instance, have deliberately provoked the fight as an excuse to kill Doyle in *apparent* self-defence?'

'Who says so?'

'We're asking you.'

'That what bloody Kevin told you, is it?'

'Had Hythe ever clashed with Doyle before today?'

'Not that I knew of.'

'You were mates, you and Doyle: teamed up as bombers, convicted together and then in the same cell block. Presumably you'd have known about any prior aggro between them?'

'I would so. For sure I'd have known.'

'More likely to know about that than, say, Kevin McGuire.'

'Here, what's that bastard been saying?'

'You would know better than him?'

'*Yes!*'

'So what about the other possibility—that someone put Hythe up to it? Any chance of that?'

'Eh?'

'Suppose Hythe was acting as a hit-man for somebody else?'

'Hit?'

'Come on, Mr Connolly, no need to look so surprised. Prison is a place characterized more by vendettas and hatreds than loyalty and love. Don't tell me Pat Doyle had no enemies.'

'Nothing. Nothing like that.'

'Like what?'

'Like you're saying. Hit-man and that. Murder.'

'He was known as General Doyle, wasn't he? Boss of the Irish faction in here?'

'Ha—hardly that.'

'Not all the villains in here are too fond of you IRA people,

are they. Suppose some lifer had had word sent in by the
Orangemen—the Loyalists—to rub out Pat Doyle? How
about that?'

'Well, if—if that's how it was . . .'

'Yes?'

'Well then, they picked the wrong target. Pat Doyle was
just a bloody peasant. Thick as a peat bog, so he was!
Calling him General Doyle—that was just a cruel joke.
They also called him Big Spud, 'cos that's the sort of brain
he had.'

DAY TWO

CHAPTER 4

'Hello, Dell. Everything all right?'

'Fine, Jack. How did you sleep?'

'Not too hot. Camp beds and all that.'

'You should have come home.'

'You know how I am with a murder. Total immersion.'

'I know you need your sleep. You miss things if you get
overtired.'

She paused, and he could imagine her sipping coffee—
fragrant, fresh-ground, Kenya blend.

'You try and get home this evening.'

'I'll see, Dell, I'll see. All right last night, were you?'

'Of course I was. No need, you know—telling Heather to
stay in. I haven't been married to the Force all these years
without being able to keep me own company.'

'She did stay in, though?'

'Of course she did. Fussing me like I was disabled.'

'She's a good girl.'

'It's what I keep telling you.'

'Yeah.'

'So what about you? Where were you last night?'

'Eh?'

'Each time I tried to 'phone you the prison switchboard said extension 308 was unobtainable.'

'Jesus . . . Well, that's it, Dell, that's the bloody nick for you. Sod's Law all the way. I'll call you this evening, okay?'

'Try and be here, Jack.'

'I'll try. Take care.'

'You, too.'

Walsh rang off, rubbing at his scalp, turning to eye his DI. 'Any sign of our deviant yet?'

Taff Roberts nodded, moving to beckon a prisoner and escort into the office.

'B–58553 Rogers, over from A Wing, sir.'

'Thank you, Officer. There's a chair outside in the passage.'

'With respect, sir, security regulations don't allow—'

'Show him the paper, Inspector. Sit down there, Mr Rogers.'

Walsh reached for the mug of vile instant coffee Taff had just brewed for them using the electric kettle in the corner —about as refreshing as the makeshift camp beds with which they had been provided the previous evening. Dell was right as usual: gone were the days when he could function effectively without regular sleep.

Walsh noticed that the slim, neatly turned out prisoner was flushed and that his hands were trembling. The hands had the familiar marks known as the Borstal Biro tattooed on the fingers: the letters L-O-V-E on the left and H-A-T-E on the right—a residue from his youth, it being near-obligatory for Borstal inmates to decorate each other with the words which had become less a message than an insignia. Similarly, tattooed across his throat was a dotted line and the words *Cut Here*. Rogers was keeping his face lowered so that it was a while before the detective realized from the movement of his shoulders that he was fighting back sobs.

'What's up?'

'It . . .' Tony Rogers leaned forward to fumble a tissue from a packet on the desk and hide his face. 'You see, it's my fault.'

'What is?'

'Poor Ronnie. It's my fault he's in all this mess.'

The argument, as usual in the ITN newsroom, was a lot less private than Kate could have wished, what with the inevitable copy-taster, researchers and so on milling around the big circular table over which their editor and master presided like a media deity, it was certainly too public to risk revealing her plan to try and make contact with a certain bright-eyed DI currently investigating inside the prison itself.

'I tell you, we're looking at the tip of an iceberg with this one, Lawrence.'

'Which is about all we ever look at with Home Office stories.' Then, persisting over her protests: 'I grant you, it made a good lead story last night: violence in the lifer wing; police marksmen out; use of those Mufti thugs; a death. It might just make the lead for part two tonight, depending on what the Home Secretary says about it in the Commons this afternoon—assuming he says anything at all. But as for—'

'Lawrence! You're being defeatist.'

'Whereas you, my sweet, are being your usual pushy self. Which is as it should be. Editors exist to be hated, reporters to find challenges. Every morning you burst out in a colossal great Promethean lather, only to have your pretty bowels torn out by your loathsome adversary of an editor.'

'Not only defeatist but patronizing.'

'Sure. And if we didn't need and deserve each other, we'd have parted company years ago.'

Kate paused long enough to count up to ten before:

'Lawrence, old thing, regardless of the Home Secretary, I want a four-minute special this evening.'

The editor heaved back in his chair and reached for the first of the five mini-cigars he allowed himself each day. It was, after all, the hour of haggling, if not with Kate Lewis, then with one or other of ITN's prima donnas trying to sell him on their particular topic at a time of day when the options were still largely open and when, provided nothing unforeseen happened to break—nothing dynamic like a terrorist hi-jack or a royal death or an oil embargo—it was sometimes possible for him to pencil in a special and allocate a VT team to cover it.

'Did you talk to Steven?'

'Not yet.'

'Let him in on it, Kate.'

'All right. All in good time.'

The editor knew that her relationship with Steve Smith, the deputy programme editor on home affairs, was far from easy. For one thing, Kate preferred to work as a loner, cultivating her own personal contacts, shielding her informers, grooming her spokesmen. Moreover, she maintained that Steven Smith was politically partisan, forever trying to impose a slant on stories—a gross professional affront to Kate for whom objectivity was all. Slants, viewpoints, bias—these were for proprietors to reflect in editorial policy—privileges to be imposed downwards by paymasters, not upwards by reporters or deputy editors whose province it was to deal in facts.

'So what are you offering for this special?'

'The wife of an A Wing prisoner who rang the office earlier.'

'Saying?'

'That the riot was inevitable. That her husband predicted it almost a month ago. That it was deliberately provoked by the prison staff.'

*

'Please, you've got to believe me, what Ronnie Hythe did to that ape Doyle, it was an *accident*.'

It had taken several minutes and a cup of instant coffee to restore Tony Rogers to a semblance of calm. Walsh was still unsure how genuine the catharsis of guilt really was. Yet whatever the prisoner's tendency to histrionics, there was clearly a tide of distress running in Tony Rogers.

'I promise you, I know Ronnie—know him better than anyone else in here. I mean, him and me, we've talked, you see. We've discussed every last detail of what he did.'

'Did when?'

'Well, to that cowing bloody wife of his. Everything. And believe me, Ronnie is not a bad man. He's *not*. You see, in a sense it wasn't really Ronnie who killed her so much as —well, as *them*: Phyllis and Sheila. All right, of course you can say—as in fact the law said at his trial—that those two bitches are *in* him, part of him, part of his personality. The female element which is said to lurk in all of us, yes? But it's them—they're the ones who drove him to it. Through jealousy, I suppose. Taunting him, whispering it at him, goading him into it—into doing away with her. Tragic, of course. Horrid. But the point is, thanks to all the help he got at Grendon and since then from me, well, they've *gone*. Phyllis and Sheila, both gone. He hasn't heard a word from them in months now. So there it is, you see: he's cured. There's nothing bad in him—not any more. He's kind, he's gentle, a very sensitive person. And—and—and no way could he possibly have intended what happened. No way. You have to believe that. I mean, at the most, if it happened the way everyone's saying, then it was self-defence. Simply hitting back at that ape Doyle. And—and like I was saying, if it wasn't for me, poor Ronnie wouldn't have been there in the first place. No way.'

Walsh sat back, his eye caught by the tattooed message: *Cut Here* . . . God alive, what an age!

'You reckon it was your fault then? How come?'

'You see, it was only because of me that Ronnie went along there—went looking for me.'

'Looking in the recess, you mean?'

'Yes. You see, during the riot, I ran into that fiendish little teaser, Jason. I was down on the Twos near Jason's peter—his cell, I should say—and he whistled me across. Of course I should have *known*. Shameful. All the excitement, I suppose. Anyway, the moment I was inside his cell with him, the randy little fiend slammed the door. Monster!'

'So that you were locked in together?'

'*Yes!* And poor Ronnie searching for me, going out of his mind . . . until, up in that ghastly recess along from my cell . . .'

'Tony, how do you know what happened up in that recess?'

'How? Everyone knows. The whole wing. The whole nick by now. It doesn't take long for word to get around in this place, you know.'

'All we know is that once the Mufti officers had retrieved control, they got everyone banged up in their cells.'

'Oh yes? Had themselves a bit of sport first, didn't they.'

'Sport?'

'Naturally they'll call it cell checks—for security. Well, if security means charging into every peter in the block and smashing up everything in sight, most of the cons as well— well then . . .'

He grimaced in irony, baring his arms to show the livid welts of bruising, then bowed forward to show how he had been shielding his head from blows. 'I was luckier than Jason. He was in a horrid mess. Him and half the block.'

'If you start a riot like that, you've got to expect some over-reaction and reprisals.'

'*We* didn't start it!'

'Whether you did or not, that's not our business, Mr Rogers. All I'm asking you is how the grapevine manages to function when you're all banged up in your cells.'

'We've had tea and slopping out since then, you know. Quite a few of us have had exercise. They can't refuse us those. Food, hygiene, exercise—they're all part of our rights under the convention.'

'And that's how you heard about Ron Hythe fighting with Doyle? During exercise?'

'I heard it from the officers first.'

'Oh? Which ones?'

'The landing officers who supervised the delivery of tea. So far as I know, they told everyone.'

Kate tried to conceal her impatience as, keeping one eye on the clock and the other on the studio floor manager, she tried to reassure the anxious Mrs Janner of total anonymity.

'No need to worry . . .'

'Listen, dear, there's plenty of screws in that nick who know me from when I go to visit Jimmy. It just needs one to recognize me on the Box and that's him done for.'

'But you see, with the studio lighting behind you, your face'll be completely dark. Just look at that monitor screen there while I sit in your chair. See—just a dark outline. Unrecognizable.'

'I just hope so, dear. I really do.'

Kate Lewis refrained from asking her why, if it was all so wildly risky for her husband, she had telephoned ITN in the first place and then agreed to come and tape an interview at the studios. Most often, when informants rang offering the 'true facts', it was because they had an axe to grind.

Being responsible media people, answerable to the Press Council, much less the laws of libel, Kate and her editor usually tried to inform the 'other side' of the claims and accusations made in the interview, if only to try and heat up the controversy.

With this one, Kate Lewis had been careful to verify that

Mrs Janner was indeed the wife of the Jimmy Janner serving life in Brentford for the shooting of a Securicor guard. That she had taken a dislike to the brassy, pugnacious forty-year-old with dyed hair and over-tight costume was neither here nor there. Doubtless Mrs Janner now felt threatened by the studio atmosphere, by the combination of cluttered technology and anonymous technicians. No doubt she was also genuinely anxious to avoid identification so as to shield her husband from staff reprisals. What bugged Kate, as always when she felt she and ITN were being used, was *why*.

'Janner-Lewis: Take One.'

LEWIS: Your husband is currently a prisoner in Brentford?

JANNER: He is, yes.

LEWIS: Serving a life sentence, which means he is in A Wing, scene of yesterday's riot.

JANNER: A Wing, yes.

LEWIS: You've said you wish to remain anonymous. Would you please explain why.

JANNER: You see, my old man told me during me last few visits how that riot yesterday was inevitable 'cos it was being set up, deliberately provoked by the prison officers. Well, being as my old man's innocent and currently appealing against his conviction, he'll be doubly at risk of reprisals if I'm identified.

LEWIS: Reprisals for what?

JANNER: Well, for this lot—for me blowing the gaff about the riot.

LEWIS: Viewers will of course realize that nothing you say can be taken as proved because at best it is hearsay evidence stated to you by your husband.

JANNER: It's nothing less than the truth, Miss Lewis.

LEWIS: Hearsay, none the less. So may we hear what he told you?

JANNER: For starters, back in the summer, he said how

the officers were giving them a wind up—getting a lot of
aggro going on the wing.

LEWIS: How exactly?

JANNER: Scores of ways. Petty things, some of them, but
others that really cut deep. Like one of the worst, which
I *can* prove, was when they cut down on visit times.
They've got to allow at least half an hour per man each
month. But it was always a fact that if you got there on
the dot of nine-thirty during a weekday, you could reckon
on as much as an hour and a half together. Then suddenly
the officers chopped it to half an hour and not one second
longer. More, they started giving all of 'em a spin—that's
a full strip search—after each visit. Then, on top of that,
they started having a full cell spin—every cell in the block
searched top to bottom. And always they'd be sure and
leave it like a right old tip: photos torn down, radios
smashed, cushions ripped open, mail and diaries all poked
into. Oh yes, then there was the aggro over censorship.
That really used to wind my old man up something rotten,
me and all. See, whenever we wrote letters to each other,
they'd be sat on by the censors for weeks. And worse than
that, they'd tell each other what we'd writ and then the
officers'd be coming round the cells and taunting the
blokes with personal details: 'Girlfriend's sent you a Dear
John, then . . . Sounds like the missis has got another one
up the spout, then . . .' Snide bloody carry-on like that.
Then another thing the officers got up to, they was all
the time looking for excuses to knock out the prisoners'
privileges: someone burnt out the hot-ring, no more fry-
ups; the element's gone in the kettle, no more brew-ups;
the telly's on the blink, no more viewing of an evening.
Another trick he said they'd pull was planting dope and
homemade weapons and that before the cell searches so's
they could get blokes busted into the seg wing.

LEWIS: Segregation wing? The punishment block?

JANNER: Right.

LEWIS: And your husband saw this as all part of a deliberate campaign of harassment?

JANNER: Miss Lewis, it had to be. A deliberate wind-up so as to push 'em into retaliating.

LEWIS: You mean actually pushing them to riot?

JANNER: Mind you, at first the blokes tried appealing: to the wing governor, to the prison governor, to the board of visitors, even to their MPs.

LEWIS: To no effect?

JANNER: None. Oh, everyone promising to look into it, but no one getting any results. Okay, so then some of 'em tried to get organized—tried to set up a petition. And that's when the Table Sixers got moved.

LEWIS: Sorry? Who got moved?

JANNER: They moved the blokes who used to sit together on Table Six. They was like the inner cabinet. Anyone wanted to start anything or get hold of anything or sort someone out, they'd have to clear it first with Table Six.

LEWIS: Presumably at a price?

JANNER: According to my old man, they wasn't extortionists. Fair rates for everything. And in return, order on the wing.

LEWIS: The alternative being anarchy—the law of the jungle?

JANNER: Right, Miss Lewis. Which is what happened the moment they took the Sixers out. All of 'em ghosted out the same night; all whisked off to different nicks around the country. Result: anarchy. That's when my hubby finally knew what the screws was up to. That's when he told me there was no other way but for the lid to blow.

LEWIS: Did he have any idea why the officers should want that?

JANNER: Obvious, Miss Lewis, innit. Pay rates, staffing ratios. Their union negotiations is all to do with *security*. Well, there it is: yesterday they proved their point. Or at least, several hundred poor bastards like my husband was pushed into proving it for them.

Tony Rogers was barely out of the incident room before Hythe's welfare officer arrived—a tweedy, middle-aged representative of the probation service with deep-set eyes and a halting, confidential manner.

'It has to be said, gentlemen, that Ronnie Hythe is in a bit of a state this morning. Reasonably so, I suppose, since he's the target of what could be extremely grave allegations.'

He paused, his gaze shifting hopefully from Walsh to his DI before again resuming to Walsh: 'As his welfare officer, I felt obliged to remind him of his rights, principally relating to legal representation. He—er—he asked me to contact his solicitor, Mr Geoffrey Spink, as a matter of urgency.'

'Fair enough.'

'Quite. Yes. You see, I don't want to give the impression of partiality here. I'm foremost an officer of the court, of course, but also with responsibility for the client's interests. Mediator, really.'

'Quite so, sir.' Walsh's expression was bland, yielding nothing, waiting for the catch. 'We'll be sure and keep you informed.'

'Thank you, yes. However, well, there is one point you might enlighten me on here and now. It—er—it's the matter of a caution. Purely procedural, I dare say. However, given these eyewitness verbals alleging assault, a caution must clearly precede the taking of any formal evidence or statement.'

'He'll be cautioned, sir, the moment we find evidence to justify it and not before.'

'Of course, I can see it must be tempting, given that Ronnie Hythe's anyway in custody, to disregard Judge's Rules here. No need to remand or even charge a prisoner until you've got really solid evidence against him. My sole concern is in regard to the—er—propriety of his interrogation and . . .'

'Quite so, sir.' Walsh stood up. 'Much obliged for your help.'

Taff Roberts made a note of the welfare officer's extension number, showed him out and then turned to Walsh.

'He's got a point though, guv'nor. Judge's Rules or not, we should have cautioned him.'

'Not something to be rushed, lad. My bet is, the moment he's cautioned, we'll lose him—he'll go dumb on us again.' Then grinning in irony: 'Reckon we should charge him as well while we're at it, do you?'

'Like the probation man just said, guv'nor, what's the hurry? He's not going to run away.' Then, when his chief continued to stare quizzically at him: 'Yeah, well, if you're asking me, no, I didn't rate much to either of those verbals.'

'Just because they're Irish . . .'

'No, guv'nor, come on, seriously now. Both of 'em were phoney as hell by my book, both lying in their teeth.'

'But what about Hythe? Did you believe *his* version?'

'Lord knows! Shifty little blighter. But—well, perhaps in balance . . .' He shrugged, reluctant finally to commit himself, unhappy with the whole feel of it.

'I told you, eh,' Walsh grunted, his teeth showing in a grin. 'Nick jobs are never straight. Never.' He shook his head, then indicated the telephone. 'Okay, get us the mendacious McGuire back over here—let's see how he reacts to the lies Connolly told us.'

Roberts dialled the wing extension and asked the duty Security Officer for McGuire to be escorted across. He was told to hold a moment, waited a longish pause and then reacted with a grunt of amazement.

'I've got Pelham here, the wing governor,' he said, covering the mouthpiece. 'Apparently McGuire was transferred out this morning. Now on his way to Albany Prison in the Isle of Wight.'

CHAPTER 5

'Mr Pelham, McGuire is a key witness.'

'I know that. I thought of querying it with you when the movement order came through.'

'So why didn't you?'

'Frankly, I thought they must have informed you. I knew you'd interrogated him last night. I presumed you'd got a full statement and . . .'

'Well, you were wrong.'

Walsh caught Roberts's look and covered the mouthpiece. 'This is a madhouse, not a prison.'

'Sod's Law, guv.'

'*Right*.' Then, resuming into the phone: 'Who authorized this movement order, Mr Pelham?'

'P-Three, as usual. Section Three of the Prison Department at the Home Office.'

'When?'

'The order's dated end of last week.'

'So how come he was still here this week?'

'The procedure is that P-Three decide on the dispersals. They send the orders on to us. Then our admin people arrange transport as and when they can. For Isle of Wight dispersals like this, it's usual to wait until there's a full batch of prisoners for transfer. Enough to fill a security van.'

'So how long ago did McGuire's van leave?'

'A good couple of hours ago.'

'And how do I get that van turned around?'

'Goodness . . .'

'There has to be a radio link. It shouldn't be that impossible.'

'Obviously, Mr Walsh, that's for the governor to decide.'

'Obviously.' Walsh nodded for Roberts to dial the governor's extension on the other phone. 'Thank you, Mr Pelham.'

'Er—as I recall, you wanted to question the officers responsible for the—er—incident with Doyle's body.'

'The stretcher clowns, yes.'

'One of them's due on shift this afternoon if you'd like him over. Name of Binton. Discipline Officer Angus Binton.'

'As soon as he arrives, please.'

Roberts handed the other phone across as Walsh rang off.

'Governor's secretary, Miss Horn. She says the governor's unavailable.'

'Detective Chief Superintendent Walsh here, Miss Horn. Where can I contact him?'

'I'm afraid Mr Hanford's on his way to the Home Office, sir.' Then, at Walsh's groan of frustration: 'I'll put you through to Mr Williams, the deputy governor.'

Williams, although he managed several sympathetic grunts as Walsh protested the loss of his chief witness, offered little hope of retrieval.

'Once the transit officers have taken responsibility for them, those prisoners are outside our authority. In effect, they're in limbo until they arrive at their new prison. You'll have to take it up with P-Three—try for a movement order back here from Albany.'

The speculation bouncing around with the football in the recreation space between A and B Wings that morning focused most avidly on Doyle's death. It was noted, endlessly, that the version of it which incriminated Hythe had been spread around by the landing officers. That in itself made it deeply suspect. Indeed, it seemed to confirm that it must have been one of the Mufti officers who had done the killing.

As for the apparent evidence against Hythe by the two IRA witnesses, no one gave that too much credence. Even Irishmen wouldn't be so thick as to risk testifying against a screw. There was a proud tradition of *esprit de corps* among the gaolers, who were sure to close ranks and stand together in face of such a situation, resistant both to physical assault and criticism . . . and moreover, likely to spread counter rumours when necessary for self-protection.

Thus the speculation in the exercise area was less to do with *who* had killed Pat Doyle so much as *why*. To some it was quite simply a case of routine brutality which had gone too far. The most popular alternative, however, was that the Mufti officer, or even Hythe for that matter, had been acting as a hit-man on a contract put out on Doyle by the new Table Sixers as a warning to the Irish Mafia. A close second to this was the theory that Doyle had been a turncoat who had grassed IRA secrets to British Intelligence, thus earning himself an execution warrant from Dublin . . . or that he had been trying to horn in on the drugs market and had got so greedy he had to be snuffed . . . and so on, in the best of prison-grapevine traditions.

'Officer Binton, sir.'

'You were on shift in A Wing yesterday afternoon?'

'Yes, sir. Subject, of course, to the disruption.'

Although he didn't actually click his heels, the smartness of his blue serge uniform, the forward set of his peaked cap, and the formal correctness of his stance, all fortified Walsh's impression that in the past Binton must have seen military training. Well set up physically, he clearly kept himself in excellent trim, was light on his feet, bright of eye and, from the crispness of his replies, also of mind. A man of energy, an athlete, a most superior being.

'We were unable to commence shift proper until after the intervention of the Mufti.'

'And your duties were then very different from usual, hm?'

'Very, sir. I was detailed for stretcher work, shifting the more severely injured.'

'Detailed or volunteered?'

'Both, in effect, sir. Volunteered and, as a consequence, detailed.'

Walsh noticed that his DI, seated to one side and hence outside the witness's eyeline, was registering contempt—presumably because, Welshman that he was, Taff Roberts was generally as intolerant of formality as he was of red tape. Welsh also was his young DI's sense of egalitarianism, the lad being as unimpressed by rank as by mystique, and generally most sceptical of those in the professions.

Although the conviction rate notched up by him and his CID mates was scored almost entirely from among those labelled as the criminal classes, Walsh knew that Taff Roberts had no illusions about the integrity of the wheeler-dealer gents in the boardrooms of the City or even of many among the ranks of those such as lawyers who were sworn to uphold the laws of the realm.

While Binton was no more of the City boardroom than of the Inns of Court, there was about him that air of rectitude and propriety which somehow implied complicity in the system.

'Care to tell us about it, Mr Binton?'

'By *it*, sir, am I right in assuming you mean the cock-up over the deceased?'

Walsh nodded, surprised that a man who clearly prided himself on his competence and efficiency should so readily concede to a blunder.

'I was teamed up with Officer Kedge, the pair of us going at it on the double to get them cleared down to where the medics had set up on the Ones. Tough going and all. By the time we reached the Fours, we were getting pretty knackered—Kedge worse than me, being as he doesn't keep himself too fit. Along to the north end recess where we found Hythe groaning on the floor and holding his head. Beside him he'd got Doyle lying there as well, to all appearances unconscious. On to the stretcher with him, strapping on, doubled back along the landing, started down the stairway.'

Binton paused to breathe in before raising himself to his fullest height and then rocking slightly back on his heels. The impression was of a man bracing himself for a confession; yet Walsh had the feeling it was somewhat staged.

'Two mistakes, sir, both of them mine. The first was to let Kedge take the lower end when he was already bushed and we'd got such a great bull of a man on the stretcher. Second was the strapping. With all the rush, I'd failed to buckle the top strap correctly.'

Again he paused, again repeating the intake of breath, the rising and settling back.

'Outcome of it was, we'd hardly started down the stairs when Doyle's top end started to slither sideways. I called out to Kedge and tried to drop my end down so as to block his fall against the banisters. But Kedge—to be honest, I don't know what he thought he was doing. He panicked. He let go with his one hand. That got it tilting and starting to come down at him. He tried to hold on, but what with Doyle's weight . . . well, the end of it was that Kedge fell back and Doyle took a purler all the way down to the Threes.'

Another pause, briefer this time, before: 'I blame myself, sir, like I said. The buckle, for one thing. And even with that, if I'd just put myself at the lower end, I'd have made a better job of catching him once he started to go.'

'So Doyle whacked down on to the Threes. What then?'

'Kedge wasn't in too good a shape. He'd taken a bit of a knock. I had to call up one of the landing officers. Then, while we're getting Doyle strapped back on, I noticed how his head was flopping around pretty odd. Took a closer look and realized, dear Christ, he's *dead*. Give us a rare old turn, that did, believe you me.'

'You thought the fall had killed him?'

Binton nodded, breathing and rocking, his expression one of studied grimness. 'You can imagine our relief when we finally got him down and the medic told us he must have been dead all along. Dead when we first got to him up in the recess.'

'And then?'

'To be honest with you, sir, I was so shook up—shocked, you know, what with thinking the fall must have killed him —I came over very odd. Had to take a break for a cup of tea before I could really get myself together.'

Was he really the type, Taff Roberts wondered. Surely it would take more than that to shake up a tough, cocksure customer like this one.

'Thank you for your help, Mr Binton.' Walsh stood up, moving round the desk. 'We'll walk over with you to A Wing.'

It was not until they were outside and nearing the inner security barrier that Walsh asked casually: 'Did you by any chance serve in the Falklands campaign?'

'No, sir.'

'But you have seen military service, hm?'

'Only as a youngster, sir. Not my scene. Far more job security in the prison service.'

'It's certainly a growth industry.'

'That's right, sir. No shortage of villains to lock away— not so long as you gentlemen keep yourselves busy.'

'Dynamic piece you taped from the Janner woman.'

'Praise indeed, Steven.' Kate Lewis pulled a wry face. 'Lawrence wanted to cut it down, of course. He's offering to nominate it as feature of the month.'

'Oh dear.' Steve Smith grimaced. 'It certainly won't endear us to the prison staff.'

'Will that worry you, Steven?'

He grinned, wagging a finger at her. Tall and gaunt, with keen, deep-set eyes above an untrimmed beard, he was, Kate had to concede, not entirely unattractive, albeit in a rather haggard, family-man way.

'So far as I'm concerned, Kate, the Prison Officers' Association are a shower of brutish chauvinists. Which is why, after Lawrence told me to take a look at the Janner tape, I chased around and made contact with a Comrade Tanner, Brentford's POA commissar.'

'Well, bully for you. Where do I call him?'

'Kate, love, knowing your passion for facts . . .'

'You thought you'd just call him yourself. Bloody fantastic. What did he say?'

'Nothing for quotes, in fact, but he was predictably scornful at the suggestion of a conspiracy of provocation by the A Wing officers. In fact, he laughed at it. He said that since *all* prisoners' wives are always convinced their husbands are the victims of malicious persecution by the staff, it was on the cards you'd find one who'd rush in front of the cameras and claim that the officers had conspired to generate yesterday's riot.'

'Glib bastard.'

'No doubt that's why he's on the POA's national executive and their number one trouble-shooter.'

'Did he get glib about anything else?'

'As it happens, yes. Exclusively for background use, of course, but he told me that the police have got statements from two IRA bombers, both of them incriminating a lifer called Ronald Hythe. According to them, Hythe and Doyle got into a desperate scrap, and Hythe killed him by accident.'

'Did he say why they were fighting?'

'Apparently, what the prisoners are saying is that Doyle was a great one for nonce-bashing. Nonce is apparently an abbreviation for *nonsense*—prison slang for nutters like child-killers and multiple sex freaks. He said nonces are always prime targets during riots; and he claims that nearly half yesterday's serious hospital cases were victims of nonce-bashing.'

'I bet it wasn't just the prisoners who were bashing them.'

'Sure. Anyway, it seems Doyle was a big butch type himself who'd been chasing around with his two Irish cronies hunting them down.'

'And this man Hythe is a nonce?'

'Strictly speaking, no. He's doing life for a rather grisly wife murder. But he had a year in a psychiatric prison, and also he's a homosexual. That was apparently good enough for Doyle and Co. Tanner says the other prisoners are adamant about it: the three of them cornered Hythe in the toilets on the top landing; but he fought back with sufficient desperation to break big Doyle's neck.'

Taff Roberts finished peeing, zipped up and moved across from the urinal to where his chief was staring down at the smudged remains of the chalk marks below the basins. Earlier, on the way across to A Wing, Binton had explained that it was Kedge and himself who had drawn the chalk marks. After the bungled removal of Doyle's body, they had come back up together, had worked out the rough positions of the bodies as best they could recall it and chalked the marks—an initiative which Walsh had been inclined to credit more to Binton's army background than to his training with the prison service.

'Could well have been a foot or two either way,' Binton had said. 'Same with the outline we put for Hythe's position. All a bit iffy, I'm afraid.'

Which both CID men felt applied to every scrap of evidence they had so far gathered on the jinx-ridden case.

Now, seen in the daylight, the toilet recess seemed smaller than in the shadowy light of the gas lamp: between five and six metres deep by about seven wide; three washbasins along the left-hand wall, flanked by four toilet cubicles along the adjacent outer wall and with urinals along the opposite side. The toilet cubicles offered a minimum of privacy, having only half-sized doors, none of them with locks. All of it depressingly sordid and singularly appropriate for the scene of a prison death.

The cell block itself, although still being tidied up and in need of repairs to the fittings, was much improved after the filth and stench of the previous evening: debris all mucked out, plumbing mainly restored, electrical and central-heating systems both back on.

They had seen several dozen prisoners outside for exercise, being watched over by almost as many officers. To the surprise of the CID men, some of the prisoners had started to yell at them, their shouts promptly being taken up by others at the cell window grids overlooking them from the towering Victorian block ... angry, bleak, half-heard phrases which, predictably enough, sought to attribute Doyle's killing to the Mufti officers.

From their fruitless review of the scene of the crime, the two CID men went down to the wing governor's office, which consisted of two cells knocked into one, the un-plastered brickwork of the walls painted a heavy dun colour and only partly hidden by filing cabinets and wall charts.

The sense of bleakness was added to by Ashley Pelham, who was now trying to cope with the aftermath of the riot. Apart from the repairs to the aged cell block, there was the damage to the men in his care: the injuries not only to their bodies but also to their morale . . . none of which was helped by the latest go-slow protest action commenced by the wing staff following the riot, and by now leaving many of the prisoners very hungry, unslopped-out, without exercise and obliged merely to nurse their wounds in the isolation of their wrecked cells.

Pelham, inclined by nature to be introspective, was further troubled by what he considered his failure to avert the riot itself and the violence of its suppression—his doubts sharpened by the elaborate report he was now obliged to prepare for the Board of Visitors and the governor.

'There are aspects of yesterday's trouble I feel you ought to know about.'

'In what context, Mr Pelham?'

'For one, the origins of the whole thing and hence the responsibility for it. Oh, I know your role here is to investigate the murder. It's been made very clear to me that I'm to avoid telling you anything that isn't specifically related to Doyle's death.'

'Made clear by whom?'

'The governor, of course. He's the one most at risk from any indiscretion.'

He stood up, moving to pour himself some water, then unwrapped and swallowed a pill.

'However, since it's possible to say that the riot and the use of the Mufti are inextricably related to Doyle's death, here goes.'

He frowned, toying with the tinfoil wrapper as he returned to his seat. 'The question is, how much credence to give to what McGuire and Connolly are saying about Hythe's killing Doyle in self-defence.' He gestured in apology. 'Obviously, I'd questioned them both before you arrived on the case.'

'And what credence did *you* give them?'

'Ha! Two lifers—convicted murderers—with a vested interest in shifting it on to the man Hythe?' He paused, his fingers worrying now at the blotter, straightening and re-straightening the scribbled sheets of his report.

'Supposing,' he resumed abruptly, 'supposing it *was* a Mufti officer, there's no way McGuire and Connolly would risk saying so.'

'That doesn't say much for the system of justice you operate in this nick.'

'I dare say. But it acknowledges the realities of prison as an institution. It's not a *natural* environment, you know. Nor is it a healthy one. Running a lifers' wing is an exercise in the balance of power between inmates and staff. For

heaven's sake, I'm not sat here in this room to *defend* the
system. Ten years I've served now. Long enough to see what
it does to men longterm. Men on both sides. Even the
strongest of characters brought down—reduced to less than
they were. How can one ever defend something which is so
patently indefensible? Just because I work here doesn't
mean I condone it or approve of it or—or—' He broke off,
fidgeting with the papers, unable to meet their gaze. 'If—
you see, if you're asking me who I see as most responsible for
Doyle's death, then the answer is W. J. Hanford, governor of
this place.'

CHAPTER 6

'Damn it, Lawrence, can't we at least run an edited version?'

'I suggested that to the controller, but he wouldn't buy
it.'

Kate groaned. It was times like this when she felt herself to
be most positively disadvantaged. Okay, the male reporters
were just as capable of paranoia and job insecurity, but at
least they didn't have the female dimension on top of it—
the nagging suspicion that, what with his broken marriage,
the controller plain resented women; moreover, that Kate
had only got the job because it was ITN policy to employ
a higher proportion of female reporters and, wow, what
better than to have their crime person an earnest, deep-
voiced woman!

'Lawrence, it's very good stuff.'

'It is also, as the controller pointed out, heavily biased
and, as you pointed out in the interview, no more than
hearsay. Furthermore, as Steve's POA contact said, every
prisoner's wife is chocker with grievances about short visiting hours and mail censorship and is convinced her poor

old wrongly-convicted hubby is being victimized by the screws.'

Kate was shaking her head in retaliation. She was as usual deeply ambivalent about the programme editor. On the one hand, she respected him as an able colleague who treated her to occasional late meals after work when he talked to her as an equal. On the other hand, there was that hire-and-fire distance between them and the obligation she felt to try and impress and please, in much the same way that, as a child, she had sought to please her austere father —look, Daddy, look!—had sought every day of her young life and indeed sought even now, for all that senility had long addled his mind.

'Spare a thought, Sister Anna,' the editor persisted, 'for all those millions of viewers who would have sat out there condemning your Mrs Janner, opulent wife of a murderous bank-robber. Why shouldn't she have her mail censored? Worse, why should *he* be allowed television and cooking facilities? Why shouldn't he have his cell searched? Why any privileges at all for such a bad lot? They're very punitive, you know, our great viewing public.'

'Lawrence . . .'

'All right, I concede that both the blocking of the prisoners' protests and the moving of the Table Six Mafia *could* be interpreted as sinister and provocative; but it certainly doesn't prove the officers deliberately provoked a riot as a ploy to strengthen their union's negotiating position.'

'You're a kowtowing, yes-man.'

'So next time make it easier for me to be a no-man.'

'What?'

'Next time, Kate Lewis, no matter how dynamic and sensational, keep your interview *short*.'

'A strong indictment of Hanford, yes, but one I intend to press with whoever conducts the official inquiry into the riot.'

Ashley Pelham was talking fast now, his voice high-pitched with tension, his eyes lowered over hands pressed flat on the blotter. 'Over the last few months, I've seen Hanford pursuing a policy of calculated inertia which made that riot inevitable. More, his stubborn refusal to yield in any way at all to the inmates' requests greatly escalated their bitterness and desperation.'

He paused briefly, nodding now in emphasis. 'And ultimately, his decision to send in the Mufti was ill-judged and in direct contradiction of my assessment from here inside the wing. Yes, there were staff trapped inside, but not accessible to the rioters: not in a hostage situation and not under threat. The level of destruction was already moderating when he sent in the Mufti. Given time, the ring-leaders would have accepted the futility of their situation and capitulated. I told him that repeatedly over the telephone. But instead he sent in the bully-boys—with the result that both the damage to cells and the level of injuries and suffering to the men was hugely increased. Moreover, Patrick Doyle died, so it is claimed, in the resulting panic.'

The wing governor paused, his hands forsaking the blotter to remove his glasses for a vigorous polish as he continued: 'So far as I'm concerned, that makes Hanford responsible. I appreciate that it's largely outside the scope of your investigation. I profoundly hope that whoever runs the riot inquiry will have the integrity to condemn him for it. Knowing the ways of Whitehall, however, I doubt they will. More probably they'll simply shunt him sideways into some admin role in the prison department.'

You and all, Walsh thought, unless you've got the backing of some very powerful mates upstairs where it counts. He could well appreciate why Pelham had just gabbed it all out at them—the anxieties of a man faced with censure and recriminations, aware that his career is under extreme threat. But, as he had said, it was way outside the scope of their investigation, and that was that.

He made a move to leave, anxious that neither he nor his DI should become in any way involved in what was clearly going to develop into an extremely bitter conflict of interests. He was barely on his feet, however, before Roberts-the-Welsh surprised him by breaking convention and wading in with a question.

'Sir, you said Mr Hanford's been into a policy of calculated inertia. Why?'

'Out of sympathy with the officers—both with their pay negotiations and, extending from that, with their complaint about the psychopaths.'

Pelham moved across to indicate a wall chart listing the name of each prisoner alongside his cell number. 'You see how a good few of the names listed have this little star marked against them? That signifies an inmate who is mentally disturbed—most of them acute criminal psychopaths. There was a time when most of these would have been in one of the DHSS special hospitals such as Broadmoor. However, the shrinks in their wisdom have now largely given up on them. The prognosis for acute psychopaths is now officially negative. Their response to treatment has now been redefined as being beyond realistic help—realistic, that is, in terms of the DHSS budget. Okay, so what to do with them? Get the judges to forget about restrictive Hospital Orders and instead dump them in Scrubs or Brentford for cut-price containment.'

Walsh grimaced, turning a dour eye towards his assistant. 'Like I said to you, Inspector Roberts, more of a madhouse than a prison.'

'It's certainly getting that way,' Pelham agreed. 'Which, of course, is bitterly resented by the wing staff whose work becomes a lot harder and more hazardous—a factor which the POA wants acknowledged by the Home Office in the form of extra training and raised status for their members.'

He paused to repeat the polishing of his spectacles, then promptly shook his head. 'I have to say it, gentlemen: it is not by chance that yesterday's riot happened to further the officers' cause, not least in the extent of its violence and also the fact that there was a death. The POA's only regret must be that your prime suspect, Hythe, is a mere schizophrenic treated at Grendon rather than a high-risk criminal psychopath.'

It was lunch-time before Harry Blake answered Kate's message, telephoning her from a pub down the road from Scotland Yard. Not that Kate had ever abused her inside contact by asking him to betray CID confidences. It was quite simply that, what with the zealousness of the Yard's public relations team, discretion ruled.

'I was hoping for something on the death of that prisoner during the riot.'

'You've got to be kidding, sweetheart.'

'Just background stuff, Harry—ideally, the chance of contacting the DI who's in there helping Big Chief Walsh on it. I think his name's Roberts.'

There was a pause while Harry thought it over. He was an officer of above-average ambition who had decided there could well be career advantages in cultivating discreet media contacts with the likes of Kate Lewis. However, as for sharing her with Taff blooming Roberts . . .

'Just how is background going to help you?' Then, before she could flannel out a reply: 'Those two—Roberts and his chief—they've got problems enough without wanting to take you on board. I mean, look at all the nonsense they've got running against them at Brentford: prison restrictions, screws, cons—it's got to be a wasps' nest. Everyone either close as an oyster or else lying their canary heads off. On top of that, a lot of pressure coming down on them from all the various lobbies and opportunists—everyone watching over them, breathing down their necks.'

'You just answered your own question,' Kate laughed. 'It's got to be a great story buried away in there.'

'Buried is the word. Kate, old love, you are the very last thing they'll want to know about, believe me.'

'Oh, I believe you.' She laughed again, enjoying the haggle. Her exchanges with Harry often went like this, his pessimism and the policeman in him pulling the one way, his fascination with the media pulling the other. So far, in their three years of subterfuge, he had never fully refused her.

'So this DI Roberts—is he a mate of yours?' Another pause, Harry reluctant to confirm it. 'I saw him outside the prison. He looked rather dishy. Nice grin.'

'Oh, sure, Taff'd give you a grin. Give you more than that and all, given half a chance. The original Welsh ram.'

'Tell you what, Harry, forget the background. Just give me his home number.'

'Very funny, sweetheart. Not that he'll see much of his home while this gig's on. His guv'nor's one of the old school. Conscientious. Believes in living on the job. If old Jack Walsh runs true to form, he'll have our Taff cloistered away in that nick twenty-four hours a day.'

Kate grunted. The picture was coming clearer now; and in the centre of it a pair of hard, penetrating eyes beneath tufted eyebrows and surmounting a lean, sardonic grin.

'Just try for me, Harry,' she concluded. 'This being the age of communications, try and get a message to your mate Taff. Tell him I'm hung up on Welsh rams.'

Jack Walsh had never made top league in the game of Force politics. His weakness lay in getting too focused on the job in hand, neglecting the need to scheme and socialize, neglecting his career strategy to the advantage of yes-men like Frank Blaize. For all that, however, he was realistic enough about the business of policing—the short cuts, the compromises, the court deals; also the murkier necessities such as the hand-outs and the dependence on informers. He had survived every imaginable career threat and professional pitfall. Indeed, he had earned himself a reputation for foxiness—an image visually reinforced by those tufted eyebrows.

Walsh and his DI, returning from A Wing to the incident room, found a priority message (already a half-hour old) to contact the Deputy Assistant Commissioner Crime.

'Ring Mr Blaize's secretary and tell her I'm on my way to the Yard,' he told Roberts. 'Then try and get hold of that other stretcher man, Kedge, and check his story against Binton's.'

Distrust of switchboard operators was only part of Walsh's decision to escape back to the Yard and the privacy of Blaize's office. Long and often sour experience of career men like Blaize had taught him the prudence of a meeting within at least twenty-four hours of the start of a case. Along with a short memo in summary afterwards, such a meeting would enable him to establish any aspects of the case likely to turn naughty later on; also, more to the point, he could plant and justify the various items later to be reclaimed as expenses.

'At least this is one investigation where you're unlikely to run up too much of a bill, Jack. Prison beds, prison food; no one to be paid off.' The DACC seemed to find it all rather comic.

'Hire of a small coffee percolator would be a help, sir.' Then, to wipe the smirk off Blaize's chubby face: 'And authorization to get a prisoner witness helicoptered back up here from the Isle of Wight.'

Tersely, Walsh went on to outline how McGuire had been whisked away down to Albany Prison that morning, transferred without any reference to himself.

'Nothing sinister in it, I dare say. Apparently the P-Three movement order was already there on Hanford's desk from last week. It could simply be a matter of callous discourtesy combined with ignorance of CID investigative methods. Alternatively, it just could have been deliberate obstruction calculated to hamper my investigation.'

'Now then, Jack, don't let's go overboard. What does the governor have to say about it?'

'Nothing. He made himself unavailable. Left his deputy to give me a lot of flannel about responsibility for inmates in transit.'

'Well, at least give him the benefit of the doubt. He's had a major riot in his lifer wing; suddenly he's in the hot seat, doubtless under a lot of pressure from Whitehall.'

'Sir, all I'm asking for is McGuire back up here sharpish.'

'All! Mountains of red tape, that's what all!' Then, persisting: 'You had an extensive session with McGuire last night.'

'But since then we've come up with discrepancies via Connolly's evidence and I need to test McGuire's version against them.'

Blaize scowled through a lengthy pause before reaching for a notepad. 'I'll look into it, but why not just send Roberts off down there?'

'Sorry, sir, I need him with me.'

Blaize glanced sharply up in query but got only a nod in reiteration. If only he was more of a detective and less of a plummy-voiced desk man, Walsh thought, he'd know that to deprive an investigator of his partner was like taking away a lame man's stick—no way to go tracking down villains. But then, men like Assistant Commissioner Blaize were of the new breed dedicated to the magic of microprocessors and computer scanners, inclined to rely on technology to the exclusion of forensic talent and imagination.

'Another thing, sir. In Doyle's prison file there's a reference to a military intelligence report.' He leaned across to pencil the reference number on Blaize's pad. 'Obliged if you'd arrange priority clearance.'

'Very well—for what it's worth.'

'Sir?'

'Look, I acknowledge the virtue of leaving no stone unturned. But in such an obviously straightforward case as this . . .'

'Is it?'

'All right, there's a conflict of evidence. But only between villains: this man Hythe denying the Irishmen's version. No call to go reading anything sinister into it, just because there's an intelligence report. There'll be a similar report on every IRA man in custody. Bound to be.'

He paused, registering Walsh's resentful stare, and gestured in retaliation. 'Look, already you're using phrases like *deliberate obstruction to hamper investigations*. Don't, Jack, please. Just because it's in prison, don't let it spook you. It's a straightforward case of manslaughter: Hythe's fighting Doyle and kills him in self-defence. A nominal three years to run concurrently with his existing life sentence.'

Walsh was still staring, still resentful. 'That's your version, is it, sir?'

'Certainly the basis of the briefing that's just been given to the Home Secretary.'

'Was this the reason I had to contact you? To hear the official version of my findings?'

'If you'd got back to me quicker, I'd have been only to happy to let you brief Mr Savage for the Cabinet meeting yourself.' Then, persisting over Walsh's retort: 'Look, why all the fuss? Have you in fact any evidence to contradict that version?'

'Nothing hard as yet, sir. However, I'd just like to clarify future procedure, if I may.'

'Sorry?'

'What happens if I do find anything, sir? Do I tell you or will you tell me?'

CHAPTER 7

To the relief of the Home Secretary, the mood of the cabinet room appeared to be one of blandness rather than concern. The turn-out, given that the main item on the agenda was the Brentford riot, was reassuringly thin: the Foreign Secretary and the Chancellor of the Exchequer both off in Brussels; apologies from Defence and also Environment. And as yet no one was offering other than politely-encouraging grins. Not that Home Secretary Savage was so naïve as to draw false comfort from that. His short tenure of office, up from Education at the last shuffle, meant that this was his first main exposure in office. As a barrister, his capability could be taken for granted; what remained unsure was his ambition: whether he viewed the post merely as a prestigious stepping-stone or whether, seeing it as a destiny in itself, he would launch in with a crusader's zeal for elaborate law and policy reforms. No true Home Secretary, after all, can claim to have made his mark until he has steered yet another Criminal Justice Act through Parliament, the more radical the more memorable. In any event, ambition notwithstanding, Peter Savage could most happily have done without this hideous prison nonsense as his first real test in office.

'Whereas I wouild not, of course, seek to minimize the severity of yesterday's—er—disturbance at the prison . . .'

'Pity.'

'Er—Prime Minister?'

'Just ignore me, Peter.'

'Ah . . . well, I'm advised that a reliable assessment of the actual damage, both in material and human terms, is likely to take several days.' He glanced round for a nod from Roy Grantley who was heading his back-up team. 'It's likely to be a week before anything can be itemized with any degree of accuracy, I gather.'

'Longer the better.'

'Except, Prime Minister,' the Attorney General murmured apologetically at his fingernails, 'in view of the publicity over the death, there has to be a statement p.d.q.'

'This afternoon at Question Time,' the Home Secretary

affirmed. 'But minimal, as I say, eschewing estimates of injury and damage and stating simply that an inquiry is to be undertaken by the Chief Inspector of Prisons. Regarding the death, I'm advised that there is absolutely no evidence to date to incriminate any of the prison staff—these Mufti chaps—with the fatality. *Prima facie* evidence, in fact, that the deceased died from a blow struck in self-defence by another prisoner whom he had attacked.'

There were indications—the gentle expulsion of breath, the pious compressing of fingertips—of relief at this. The Attorney General glanced at the PM before asking: 'How solid is this evidence?'

'Well—er—actually statements from a couple of convicted IRA men. But both were close colleagues of the victim, so . . .'

'Fair enough, then. I suggest you tell the House about that, within the limits of discretion, of course.' The PM was clearly all set to get on to other matters, was indeed already reaching for the agenda sheet when the venerable, froglike Lord Chancellor rumbled into life.

'Respects, PM, but may we not hear something of the origins of this business? Also the prison governor's decision to request police marksmen and also make use of these Mufti heavies?'

Peter Savage waited for a curt nod from the boss before resuming.

'As to origins: the thrust of the inmates' complaints appears to have been twofold: on the one hand a protest at the erosion of their privileges, on the other a failure of the established complaints procedure. Moreover, I'm advised there may have been a difficulty with personalities—primarily with the governor of the prison, W. J. Hanford.'

He paused to glance round again at Roy Grantley so as to attribute the source of this advice.

'It appears Hanford is a tough disciplinarian, in contrast to the wing governor's—er—leniency. Whether or not Hanford has been deliberately provocative, that is what the inmates were claiming. In effect, their sit-in was a *Hanford Out* thing—clearly something which, if he was to retain authority, he had to resist. That resistance precipitated the riot, which in turn, Hanford being somewhat of a gung-ho type, led to his rushing in the cavalry.'

Savage paused, but no one laughed. He took a hurried sip of mineral water and cleared his throat. 'Regarding the deployment of police marksmen, I understand Hanford asked for them as a precaution against any armed external presence.'

'Such as who, Home Secretary?'

'Well, sir, I believe against the possibility of the whole disturbance having been set up as part of a coordinated escape attempt by, say, the IRA element.' He paused for another sip before resuming. 'As for his use of the Mufti, I'm advised that he may in fact have sent them in against the advice of the wing governor who, although among the staff trapped inside, remained in telephone contact with those outside. None the less, it is a Category A security prison, and A Wing has a concentration of extremely danger-ous individuals, including not only the IRA terrorists but also a high proportion of psychopaths; furthermore, there have been several nasty examples of riot-cum-hostage situa-tions elsewhere—factors which Hanford is, I gather, citing in justification for ordering a pre-emptive strike before the situation inside the wing could deteriorate to a point where the trapped staff were put more seriously at risk.'

'Harry Blake speaking, Taff. This a good moment for a word in your ear?'

'Accepting the unfailing lack of privacy in prison, why not?'

'Oh gawd. Like that, is it?'

'Sod's Law all the way, Harry.'

'Anyway, I know your guv'nor isn't there because I just

saw him here, chewing his way through a steak up in the canteen.'

'That's bloody loyalty for you! Leaves me here to eat porridge while he slinks off for a nosh-up at the Yard.'

'Listen, I'm just putting this your way in case you're interested. It's no sweat to me whether or not you follow it up.'

'So get on with it.'

'See, it's about this bird who fancies you.'

'Christ sake, Harry! I'm stuck here in purdah on this pig's ear of a case, old Jack Walsh working himself up to an ulcer, and you start pimping on about some bird.'

'Taff, her name's Kate Lewis. She saw you arrive there yesterday evening, said to tell you she's hung up on Welsh rams and wants to meet.' He paused, waiting for a response, thrown by the silence. 'Taff?'

'She's a friend of yours, right? Someone you—er—*talk* to quite often?'

'In a manner of speaking.' Harry had already decided he could trust his fellow DI's discretion over informal media contacts. 'Very up-market, very special.'

'Okay, no need for the sales talk.'

'Her home number's 348-7431. Unattached and *very* discreet.'

'But up to all the tricks, eh.'

'Ah, *only* the ones you want to play, Taff. My word on that. She owes me too much to start getting clever.'

DI Roberts had a note written out for his chief when he returned an hour later.

Proposed text of the Home Secretary's statement to the Commons. If we want to suggest any revisions, the PR chief'd like 'em now-now.

Walsh took the note, glanced through the text then handed it back without comment, turning instead to start unpacking an electric coffee percolator he'd brought with him.

'Er—guv'nor, they're a bit tight for time. Although he's not due to spout until three-thirty, they're getting a press release out in advance and . . .'

'The Secretary of State'll say what's in there regardless.'

Walsh discovered there was no electric plug on the percolator's cable, swore, and moved to pick up the telephone as he continued: 'Anyway, he's not saying anything untrue: we *are* questioning a prisoner.'

'But this bit here—no evidence to incriminate prison staff?'

'Look, lad, politicians aren't concerned with precise truths which'll stand up to cross-examination. Let him bend it. Happen it might mean we get a bit more cooperation from the officers.'

'But, guv . . .'

'It's no skin off our nose if it turns out to be wrong. They wrote it, not me.'

'But if we don't query it now, then we . . .'

'Taff boyo, we've more important things to do than haggle with politicians.' He gave up waiting for the switchboard, banged down the telephone and waved the percolator cable at his DI. 'Like where the hell do we get a plug for this thing?'

ITN's lobby correspondent, having got the advance on the Home Secretary's statement from the Whitehall press office, rang straight through to Kate Lewis.

'It's all predictably bland. Noncommittal to the point of evasion. Nothing specific on injuries or the extent of damage; official inquiry by CI Prisons—i.e. internal, keeping it all nice and cosy.'

'What's he saying about Doyle's death?'

'Prison staff provisionally exonerated . . . a prisoner is being questioned . . . although not as yet charged with any offence, would not want to prejudice the course of justice with premature release of information . . . will, of course, keep the House fully informed of further developments.'

'Did you pick up any background vibes from anyone?'

'Not at Westminster. But it's obvious there's a high-level flap going on at the Home Office. Philip Knowles is keeping a tight clamp on the PR side, and apparently he's working directly to the senior mandarin, Roy Grantley. My most reliable Whitehall contact, usually most forthcoming, has made herself firmly unavailable. The lobby man on the *Telegraph* reckons they've all been told to play dumb and blame it on the purge Downing Street's ordered on Civil Service leaks.'

'What purge?'

'That's what I asked him. He didn't know. Which seems to apply to everyone I've spoken to: no one knows a blessed thing.'

'Typical Home Office hush-up.'

'No, Katie, this is tighter than usual—suspiciously so.'

'Time I met this boss-man, Hanford.'

'Just you, guv?'

Walsh nodded, moving to the door. 'We don't want to pile in mob-handed. You stay here and hold the fort.'

Roberts allowed a minute after he was alone and then picked up the telephone to dial the number Harry had left him. Strictly exploratory, he told himself; sheer curiosity to meet a real live TV personality—see if they really were real and not just animated robots.

He heard the number ring three times and then the click preceding a recorded message.

'Hello and welcome to the Kate Lewis Phone-In Show. This is not Kate Lewis speaking; this is an answering machine pretending to be Kate Lewis. But take heart. If you wait for the tone and then leave a message, the *real* Kate Lewis will contact you when she gets home.'

Taff grinned at the contrast to the austere Crime Correspondent image. It took him a moment to think up his reply.

'Er—there's a boozer down Brentford High Street called the Bag o' Nails where the original Welsh ram likes to look out for ewes of an evening.'

'Miss Horn, I know the governor's back in the prison. I'd be obliged if you'd buzz him to say I'd like a word.'

Vera Horn sighed, adjusting her spectacles. She was a mature lady with dyed ginger hair and a roguish grin which she tended to overdo. Noisy at parties, Walsh thought, a touch self-important and given to misplaced loyalty.

'Mr Hanford was most specific—'

'Not about denying me cooperation, I'm sure.'

'Of course not. Nor has he, Chief Superintendent. The authorization regarding escort officers last night; then again this morning arranging you a permanent outside phone line. As for that business over McGuire's transfer . . .'

'A matter of expediency, Mr Walsh.'

The CID man turned to where the prison governor had just emerged to stand in his office doorway. The voice had that throaty tone of a man given to excessive drinking and smoking—an impression reinforced by the pouchy eyes and the premature sag of what must once have been a powerful rugby-forward's frame.

'Not security, Mr Hanford? That's the usual excuse I seem to get in this place.'

'His own security, yes.' The governor made no move to usher Walsh into his office, his expression as obstructive as his position in the doorway. 'You interrogated him for over an hour last night, taped what he told you, then saw Hythe, then Connolly. You had every opportunity to have McGuire back in again last night or else first thing this morning, but you haven't. Meanwhile, whatever threat he was under was my responsibility so long as he remained here.'

'Threat? While he was banged up in isolation?'

'This is a prison, Mr Walsh, home to a lot of very violent and ruthless customers. I wasn't appointed to take risks with the wellbeing of those under my care.'

No, Walsh reflected with irony, nor to adopt a policy of deliberate inertia, calculated to push them into a riot. But why? If Pelham was in fact right, why provoke them like that? Was it that the days of Governor Power had now finally passed? At one time, as master of a contained and essentially oppressive regime with a rigid discipline structure, the power of a prison governor was awesome: answerable to higher authority, yes, yet isolated like the skipper of a vast ship. But now much of that power was being eroded, usurped by the men supposed to be under his command. So that now, in this particular prison, Walsh was unsure where the real balance lay, where the policies were formed and the final decisions made. Was it here in this man's office or was it in the backroom of the officers' club used by the shop stewards of the POA?

It was still possible, Walsh knew, for most governors actually to govern. Given men with sufficient tact, energy and strength of personality, they could still retain the helm and pilot their ship. Just. But was this surly, guttural-voiced, pouchy-faced individual really anything more than a puppet to more subtle hands?

'Mr Walsh, why don't you do us both a favour? Why don't you simply get on with your job and leave me to get on with mine. You've got your man—got him banged to rights—evidence, witnesses, the lot. Suppose you just leave it at that and stop snooping around beyond your authority.'

Hanford had turned, moving back into his office, the door already closing in Walsh's face as: 'And before you go listening to any more slanderous bleatings from Pelham, remember he's a desperate man whose job's on the line.'

The text of the Home Secretary's statement to the Commons stood as item one on the Brentford branch POA agenda that evening. The mood of the executive lifted visibly as John Tanner read it out, even the contentious Ned Ballard settling back in his seat with a grunt of satisfaction.

Only the branch secretary, Gerry Dancer, remained un-smiling, duly remarking that Savage's reassurances were 'owt but a typical politician's palliative.'

'All right, Gerry. But he was briefed on what he said by the copper.'

'Aye. Which puzzles me because him and his oppo must have heard the rumours buzzing around this place.'

'He's not so daft as to listen to rumours.'

'How do we know that?'

'As it happens,' Tanner reassured them, 'I did some quiet checking on friend Walsh. Thirty years in the Force. No illusions about villains. A man who's spent his life putting them away, not pleading their cause. A law-and-order man. A practical, run-of-the-mill copper who knows the rules and the way things work. Just wants to keep his nose clean and his conviction rate up. Okay?'

'And that youngster he's got tagging along?'

'Just a DI who knows his place. Loyal to his chief.'

'If they're so okay, how come they keep pushing our lads out the interview room?'

'Grow up, Gerry. You've heard the way some of those defence barristers go on: "Me lud, I submit that the questioning of this witness was grossly prejudiced by the close proximity of a prison awfficer."'

This won John Tanner a round of applause for his mimicry and cost Gerry the penance of a fresh round of jars.

'Right, then,' the trouble-shooter resumed, reaching for the agenda, 'Item two: future action—principally re the press.'

'Less said to that shower of bastards the better, John.'

'Normally, as you know, I'd agree with that. But as it happens I think I've got us quite a handy liaison going with ITN.'

'That Lewis tart? Don't trust her, mate. They're all two-faced in that racket.'

'Not with Kate Lewis, no. This bloke's deputy programme editor. He rang about an interview Lewis had taped with the wife of a con in A Wing. Malicious slander, of course. Anyway, he just rang me back to say he'd persuaded his boss to drop it.'

'He what?'

'The interview won't be screened.'

'You're not married then, Kate?'

'Not any more, no.'

Actually to meet up together in the Bag o' Nails had come first as a surprise, neither having really given it much credence, and now increasingly as a relief at discovering their affinity.

'You know, you should do us all a favour and smile a bit more on the Box.'

'Oh, that's not me. That's someone else in front of those cameras.'

She could have added that it was a fraudulent someone else. But instead she decided that, just because he seemed sensitive and interested, that didn't mean he'd want to hear about her tedious professional hang-ups: the dichotomy between real person and screen image; the times when she wondered if the original Kathy had quietly abdicated in favour of this glib, pushy, interrogative Kate.

Oddly enough, as he told her later that evening, Taff Roberts often experienced a similar sense of unreality about his CID work, a nagging sense of irrelevance, as though he and the suspects and the villains and their lawyers were all acting out some bizarre pretence.

Right now, however, both he and Kate had the shared sense of reverting to their real selves—curiously so, since each had come in the expectation of professional gain . . . which seemed to leave a mutual chemistry as the most likely explanation. Yet if so, it was the chemistry not only of physical attraction but also of emotional need.

Although Taff was a committed bachelor, this had little
to do with Welsh ramming. That was an image perpetrated,
largely out of envy, by his CID colleagues. In fact Taff was
still unmarried mainly because of his dedication to his work
and his belief that, given the energy and time it demanded,
it was clearly incompatible with what he felt marriage should
be about . . . an impression all too often confirmed by what
he saw of the hapless, guilt-tinged marriages of his mates in
the Force. Yet, for all that, it left a need, of which the likes
of Kate most forcibly reminded him.

'The divorce was finalized last year, Taff.'

'Amicably or with aggro?'

'Let's say civilized. I suppose the recriminations were
mostly on Bill's side.'

'So there wasn't another woman?'

Kate laughed but in self-deprecation. 'Bill said there was
—me. The *other* me. The one I'd become since getting this
big-deal job.'

'So he wanted a wife and not a media personality?'

'You sound like his solicitor.'

'Sorry! This habit of asking questions.'

'Yes. An occupational hazard common to us both. The
interrogators.'

'You see yourself as big deal? The great investigative
crusader?'

'No, Taff.' She laughed again but now in pleasure, with
relief at the denial. 'I'm just another news reporter. Which
I'm sure was one reason I got the job. Crusading journalists
can be an awful pain, you know. Editors want sleuths, not
idealists.'

She paused to sip Goldener Oktober, then grinned in
irony. 'Also, luckily for me, it had just become ITN policy
to employ more women reporters.'

'Brighten up the nightly gloom and doom with a bit of
talent, eh?'

Kate grimaced but conceded a nod. It was a belief which

haunted her: you don't survive on ability, Lewis old love, but merely because you tart up the gloom.

'So what about you, Taffy Roberts? Crime crusader or plain wage-earner?'

'Oh, absolutely, yes.' He punctuated it with a grin. 'And double overtime on Sundays. Fancy another bottle?'

'Should you? I mean, if you've got to go back to work . . .'

'You're right, I shouldn't . . . Don't you have to work, too? Drunk in front of the cameras, my God.'

'Well, no.' Unexpectedly she found she couldn't hold his eyes. 'They killed my one little scoop today, and the Home Secretary's statement was so bland it left me redundant.'

'So instead, off for an evening's researching, eh?' Not that there was any hint of rebuke in his tone; on the contrary, he reached forward and touched her hand. 'All in the line of duty, eh?'

'Look, Taff . . .'

'No, no, please. No call to apologize. We both came here with our eyes open.'

He paused, trying to recall just why it was he had come but was glad that, whatever the reason, it no longer seemed to matter. 'In point of fact, there's not a lot I could tell you about the investigation even if I was allowed to. We've got a lot of doors being slammed in our faces, a lot of people putting forward conflicting points of view, the usual lies and half-truths.' He grinned, his hand still on hers. 'Much like your job at times, I imagine.'

'Right.'

'Anything you can tell me? Apart from how soon we can meet again.'

'Only a few bits of hearsay and gossip, for what they're worth.'

She went on to outline for him first the nonce-bashing theory and then the gist of Mrs Janner's claims about the riot's being a deliberate conspiracy by the prison staff. She half expected him to reject both out of hand, but instead he gave a wry shrug and then nodded.

'Okay then, Kate.' He leaned forward to give her a kiss which, although brief, none the less served as a sensual promise. 'If you want someone to back up that conspiracy notion, you could try and get hold of a very disillusioned wing governor name of Ashley Pelham. Ask the prison switchboard to put you through to A Wing. But be very sure, if you do get hold of him, not to mention me. I never told you, okay?'

Later, arriving back at the incident room, DI Roberts found his guv'nor drinking Scotch and listening to the McGuire tape.

'As it happens,' Walsh grinned, stopping the tape and sliding the bottle across the desk at him, 'there's no need for you to stick around here tonight.'

'Great.' Taff waved two fingers at him. 'Now he tells me.'

'Find yourself a bit of the other, did you?'

'A very fancy piece, as it happens, aye.' Taff poured himself a drink. 'Anyway, since I *am* back, what's new? Sod's Law as usual?'

Walsh gave a rueful grunt and nodded. 'A nice little murder to go out on, Jack. That's what the assistant commissioner told me yesterday. Patronizing bugger.'

Roberts limited himself to a sympathetic murmur. It was not usually the chief's style to voice even mild criticism of senior officers, much less unburden his frustrations like this.

'An hour ago I had His Excellency ring me from the Yard to say that Hanford's been complaining to his people in Whitehall—saying I'm exceeding my brief and impeding his efforts to restore normal prison activities.'

'Cheeky.'

'The commander in P-Five was very choked off about it.'

'And Mr Blaize? How did he take it?'

Walsh shrugged, pulling a face. In fact, he had considered

the DACC's response distinctly unsupportive. Barely deigning to hear Walsh's side, he had pointed out that Ashley Pelham was known to be engaged in a bitter vendetta with the prison governor, and anyway what relevance did he have to Walsh's investigation? As to the McGuire transfer, Hanford had acted within his authority; and in any event, to judge from the McGuire interview transcript, any further interrogation could satisfactorily be done by the local CID on the Isle of Wight. Finally, Blaize had now been shown the MoD's intelligence file on Doyle and found in it nothing of any likely significance to the man's death.

'Merely routine stuff,' Blaize had said. 'Details of his background and recruitment, training, rank, previous missions and so forth. No indication that he'd turned informer either before or after his arrest. No indication of holding senior rank. On the contrary, he seems to have been regarded by the IRA command in Dublin as mere dog's meat, he and Connolly trained up and fielded together under the command of Evelyn Glenholm, the pair of them in fact pulling off rather more bombing jobs than Dublin had expected of them before getting caught.'

Blaize had brushed aside Walsh's resentment at not seeing the intelligence report for himself, explaining that it had been delivered to him in person by a military dispatch-rider who had waited at the Yard for Blaize to read it through and then return it to him to take straight back to the MoD vaults.

'The thrust of it,' Walsh rumbled to his DI as they finished off the Scotch in anticipation of the camp beds, 'the message is, stop being so conscientious. Leave Pelham to fight his own battles, leave the Mufti to mop up their own bloodbath. You and I just get on and tie up the manslaughter case against Hythe, charge him and have done.'

Taff Roberts grunted, eyeing his chief as he drained his glass and stood up. 'Be nice if it was that simple, eh, guv.'

Walsh stared dourly back through a rather drunken

silence before also heaving to his feet. 'First thing tomorrow we'll have another go at that ferrety blighter Hythe.'

DAY THREE

CHAPTER 8

The two detectives reached the incident room next morning to find the telephone ringing: Ashley Pelham to say he'd had the prison hospital in touch with him about Ronald Hythe. The problem, as usual, was one of security in that each of the injured prisoners over in the Hammersmith Hospital had to have a couple of officers constantly present by his bedside. Naturally, the governor was anxious to get as many of them as possible back inside, which meant getting beds cleared for them in the prison's hospital.

'The doctor says it's okay for Hythe to become an out-patient and hence be moved out. But, frankly, after the McGuire business, I felt at least I should confer with you first.'

'Appreciated, Mr Pelham. The start of a new day, and already we have a new approach. When will you shift him?'

'Just as soon as we can get an escort across there.' Pause. 'One thing: the governor wants him in the segregation unit.'

'Oh? Why there?'

'He—er—he's assuming that Hythe's about to be charged, in which case it's going to be safest to segregate him over there on Rule 43—for his own protection.'

'Segregate?' Walsh's jaw was set tight. 'As I understood it, thanks to the riot, the whole of A Wing is now a virtual segregation unit—none of the cons allowed out of their cells for free association or work.'

'That's right, sir, but hopefully not for too much longer.'

'Tell you what, Mr Pelham, when the governor decides

to change them back to normal, you let me know. Likewise, *if* I decide to charge Hythe, I'll let the governor know. All right? Until then, I can see no harm in keeping him handy on A Wing.'

He could hear Pelham starting to reply, but he persisted regardless. 'Meanwhile, perhaps you'd tell the escort officer to bring Hythe in here to us for further questioning.'

They set up the tape-recorder and waited. Walsh finally got his percolator going and brewed them some Brazilian roast, so that in that particular context the day got even better. Yet still no sign of the prisoner. Eventually the DI telephoned Pelham who, after apologizing, explained that he'd just learned that Hythe's solicitor had arranged to come and see his client first thing that morning.

'Wonderful!' Walsh exclaimed as Roberts rang off. 'No bastard thinks to clear it with us first.'

'Prisoners do have rights, guv, like his welfare officer said.'

They were rights which the two CID men were to hear elaborated soon after by Hythe's solicitor.

Not that Geoffrey Spink was one of those earnest, rights-conscious lawyers who cultivate fat practices specializing in the defence of hardened criminals. Spink's prosperity, in fact, stemmed more from his familiarity with the legal-aid department of the Inner London Magistrates Court—the department favouring him with numerous clients because, as a *quid pro quo*, Spink often managed to talk the clients into pleading guilty.

He was stocky and flannel-suited, the weakness of his chin only partially concealed by a beard. His manner was that of the eternal mitigator, soft-spoken and earnestly sincere.

'Hythe wants to cooperate, Chief Superintendent, as you'll doubtless have appreciated from your interrogation in the hospital unit on the night of the incident. No, please, I'm not here to challenge the probity of what he said, for all that it was informal and *not* elicited under caution—

moreover, that you were at that stage in ignorance of Hythe's history of psychotic abnormality. No, no, all I'm asking is that you should allow for his physical state at that time— shocked and partially concussed.'

'You've talked him into changing his story, Mr Spink, is that what you're about to tell us?'

'Good heavens, no. Good gracious. But I can tell you from my handling of his previous conviction that Ronald Hythe's is a most tragic case. The victim of acute paranoid schizophrenia, you realize, in the grip of which he—er— disposed of his wife—an act over which he now feels acute remorse.'

It was on Walsh's tongue to remind the solicitor that he was not addressing himself to a bench of softie JPs. Instead he headed off further pleading by pouring the man some coffee.

'You can trust us to make a fair assessment of your client, Mr Spink.'

'Thank you. Delicious. Most welcome. The point, you see, the point I wanted to make is that, if my client was to revise certain aspects of his story—er—no, no, let's put it another way: if it so happens that, with his concussion now ameliorated, Mr Hythe happens to recall the events somewhat more clearly than before, may I take it you might allow for that in preparing your report for the prosecution department?'

'You're here to do a bit of horse-trading, is that it, sir?'

'I wouldn't want to put it as crudely as that.'

'Of course you wouldn't. However, sir, DI Roberts and I have to leave soon for a forensic conference at the Yard, so . . .'

'In short then, Chief Superintendent, if I can persuade my man to plead manslaughter, might you support that plea in your report?'

'Support it?' Walsh's face was a mask to his cynicism. 'How?'

'The framing of any charge will be based on what you report to the DPP. If you were to stress, say, the strength of the self-defence aspect, then clearly the Director would be less likely to press a charge of murder.'

There was a pause. Walsh tugged at his eyebrows, his mind ferreting through Hythe's account of the incident.

'You think you can persuade your client to revise his story, hm?'

'I can commend it to him as a realistic course of action.'

'Specifically, to lose the Samurai?'

'Pardon?'

'Retract all reference to his being whacked unconscious by any baton-wielding Mufti officers?'

'Er—well, that would certainly seem to be the area of— er—primary aberration—allowing, as we said earlier, for his concussion and, likewise, for his history of psychiatric disorder.'

Walsh disappointed his DI by standing up to reach forward and shake the solicitor's hand. 'It's a deal, Mr Spink. If your man decides to say that, I can see no reason why we shouldn't reinforce the self-defence element in our report.'

He moved round to usher the lawyer across to the door. 'We'll hold off interviewing Hythe any further until we get the nod from you. Within limits, of course. Let's say until this evening.'

Taff Roberts sighed, regretting that it had to be done this way. But there it was, foxy by face, foxy by nature. Besides, there was no disputing that this was the way things were done, the way of the world.

'Wheels within wheels, eh guv'nor,' he murmured as Walsh closed the door behind the solicitor and crossed to the telephone to dial his home number.

'We shall see, lad, we shall see.' He gave a noncommital shrug, then spoke into the telephone. 'Hello, love. It looks like I might be home tonight after all.'

*

Kate Lewis turned along the street of comfortable middle-class semis, checked the address given to her that morning by the lobby man's contact in the Home Office, then walked up the path and pressed the bell of number ten.

'Mrs Pelham? Good morning. Is your husband at home by any chance?'

'I'm sorry, no. Can I . . . ?'

'Kate Lewis of ITN. I wonder, could I possibly come in?'

Fiona Pelham was a slim, freckle-skinned Scotswoman and conscious of being not at her most presentable. She hesitated, frowning in uncertainty.

'It's about this trouble your husband's having at the prison. It's possible we can be of some help to him.'

'Oh.' The woman shrugged in resignation, stepping aside.

'How soon are you expecting him back, Mrs Pelham?' She moved through into the comfortably furnished living-room, its floor cluttered with the toys of young children. 'Do you think there's any chance of getting him home during the lunch-hour?'

'Ronald, I know what you're saying about this officer rushing in and hitting you. But can you be absolutely sure about that?'

'You're kidding me on, Mr Spink.'

'And even if you *think* you're sure, is there any way we can hope to substantiate it?'

The solicitor paused with irritation as Hythe gestured for him to keep his voice down—needlessly so, since the officer at the further end of the row of interview cubicles couldn't possibly have heard what they were saying even had he been trying to do so.

'Substantiate?'

'Prove it in a trial. The evidence of McGuire and Connolly is in direct conflict. Both of them contradicting you.'

'Well, naturally, guv. Look, they may be Irish, but they're not that thick.'

'I don't follow you.'

'Not so dumb as to give evidence against a screw.'

There was a pause, Spink realizing that he'd best switch to a less challenging approach. He offered the cigarettes he kept for such occasions, watching as Hythe fumbled eagerly to light up.

'Try,' he murmured, 'try and see it from the point of view of a jury. They'll hear McGuire and Connolly for the prosecution both swear that it was you. Then they'll hear you say how you *think* you were hit by an officer. No, no, no, please hear me out. Then, when you're cross-examined, they'll hear about your head injury, possible amnesia, psychiatric history, your voices, Janet and Sheila . . .'

'Phyllis.'

'They'll hear all that and also, inevitably I'm afraid, they'll hear about your wife . . .'

'Give it a rest, Mr Spink.'

'I'm merely giving you a realistic appraisal of the trial should you insist on this version about the officer.'

'Version? It's the *truth*.'

'Maybe, Ronald. But it is also true that, if you stick to it, you'll have to face a jury trial and possible conviction for murder. Whereas if you accept my considered advice and enter a plea of guilty to manslaughter, I'm confident we can do a deal with the prosecution and ensure a minimum sentence which will run *concurrently* with your present life sentence, so that in effect you'll be most unlikely to serve any longer in prison than you're serving already.'

'But, Mr Spink . . .'

'No, Ronald, don't let's labour it any more. I've given you my advice. I can see you have doubts. Take the day to think it over. Go away, have a lie-down in your cell and have a good think about what I've said.'

He stood up, signalling to the officer that he had concluded with his client.

'When you've made up your mind—one way or the other,

but by this evening—let the wing governor know and he'll arrange for you to see the CID officers investigating the case.'

The conference to review the forensic evidence was held at the Scotland Yard laboratory among the computer VDUs, rapid-scan microscopes, gas-chromatography analysers and the forensic technicians responsible for their wizardry. None the less, the show was dominated by the Home Office pathologist. Dr Craig's findings, however, although supported with spectacular colour photographs and path lab reports, were largely inconclusive, being related more to elimination than incrimination.

'I'm afraid about the only really positive thing I can offer is the cause of death: dislocation of the atlas and axis vertebræ due to a sharp but not excessively violent blow struck at this crucial point below the base of the left ear, either a chance contact by a fist or else a weapon such as an officer's riot stick—or else, Jack, quite possibly by the victim's falling heavily against the rim of one of those washbasins. Although all the basins were checked in vain for traces of dermal tissue or hair to test for this possibility, there had been several people around the scene of the crime who could unwittingly have smudged off any traces.

'Alternatively, we cannot eliminate the possibility that it was a deliberate blow skilfully delivered to that vulnerable point by someone trained in close combat or in one of the martial arts such as karate. A blow struck either with the edge of the hand or with a small weapon of some kind.

'Regarding these multiple abrasions received a short while *after* death, I understand you people have identified some particles which tend to confirm that the corpse managed to part company with a stretcher during removal from the top landing. Toby, I'm sure you'll have more to say about that when I'm finished.

'My examination of Doyle's corpse revealed clear evidence that he had been brawling prior to death: bruising on the knuckles, evidence of punch or kick bruises on his body and face. However, Jack, given that IRA prisoners can often become targets for violence during such riot situations, it would be dangerous to assume that these occurred during the fatal tussle which resulted in his death. Certainly, when you took me up to the ward in the prison hospital to examine his alleged assailant, this fellow Hythe, I was unable to locate the sort of injuries I'd have expected from a fight with a big bloke like Doyle. Nor, as a matter of record, could I see any sign of bruising on either of Hythe's hands, neither on the knuckles nor on the edge of the palm. Moreover, there was no thickening of the dermal tissue along the edge of the palm—a factor discernible along the palm edges of many karate practitioners. Finally, on that same point, despite minute examination of Doyle's skin at the point of impact, we were unable to locate any alien skin cells such as might have been left by a hand chop or punch.

'I'm sorry, Jack, but you see how it seems to be all negative.

'Incidentally, reverting for a moment to my physical examination of Hythe, there were similarities apparent between the blow which knocked him unconscious and that which killed Doyle: received with a similar force, from a similar weapon or else a similar fall. Had it been received —delivered—an inch or so lower down, you might well have had two corpses instead of one corpse and one suspect.

'Miss Lewis, forgive me, but how do you come to know all this about my husband?'

Kate smiled at her, reaching for one of the glasses of cider which Ashley Pelham had just poured to go with their sandwich lunch. It was at times like this, manifesting sympathy so as to allay fears, that she least liked her job. Akin to Taff Roberts, she thought, and his sense of falseness and unreality. Yet at least his work was concerned with the pursuit of justice rather than the titillation of a few million bored viewers. While it did sometimes happen that Kate's stories also served the course of justice, that aspect was seen largely as icing on the ratings cake.

'These differences your husband has been having with Mr Hanford—they're no secret among the wing staff, you know.'

Fiona Pelham was sitting very straight, her hands clasped tightly between her knees as she stared at her husband.

'And now this dreadful riot,' she said, 'bringing it all to a head.'

He reached across to touch her arm. 'Hanford's got his knife out, there's no denying that.'

'It's so *unfair*!' She turned to continue to Kate; yet the reporter had the feeling she was really speaking to her husband about the situation in which, inevitably, she too had to share. 'When he first joined the prison service it was all so different. A vocation—a Christian calling. The opportunity, you see, to help men start a new life.'

'*Dare to Care*, Fiona. You remember that?' Then, in rueful explanation to Kate: 'That was our service motto in Scotland, where I signed up in the mid-'seventies. *Dare to Care*. And at that time it still meant something. It was still official policy that criminal behaviour could be modified, the misfits taught social skills and a trade before being released as useful members of society.'

He sighed, shaking his head, but in irony and regret. It was his wife who snorted in bitterness.

'Now all the officers *care* about is more money for less work!'

'Oh now, Fiona, be fair.'

'Fair? Is it fair to use the education and training facilities the way they use them as—as a bargaining ploy in their union negotiations?'

'But the policy—that and the budget—they're still dictated from the top.' The wife went to argue, but Pelham took her hands as he persisted to Kate. 'Caring costs extra money, you see. It takes almost double the staff to try and rehabilitate a man as opposed to merely containing him. And already it's costing over £450 a week just to contain each lifer in A Wing.'

He gestured at the futility of it all. 'So there we are, you see: back to Newgate; back to the era of the turnkeys.'

'And too bad for those like you, Ashley, who joined as a vocation—those who answered a call.'

'All right, love, all right. But the question for you and me now—and it's obviously what brings Miss Lewis here today —is what I do next.'

'Ronnie, old love, welcome back!'

Tony Rogers trotted up alongside and together, their voices at a murmur, the two started into a steady jog-trot around the exercise area. Normally, they'd have sat around chatting and feeding the pigeons; but now, following the riot, things had changed.

'How's that head of yours?'

'Throbbing like a hard-on, mate.'

'Yeah? Rather walk, would you?'

'No, Tony, no.' He gestured around. 'They're all watching me.'

'The screws?'

'Everyone. Screws, Table Six, the Micks, all of 'em. But the screws the most. They killed little Butch. Blood and feathers all over my peter.'

'Yeah? Rotten bloody swine. Listen, Ronnie, you mustn't let them worry you. Honest. Since the riot they're keeping us all banged up tight as a drum. No labour, no association. Nothing but double Valium all round. The screws are on a go-slow, but just the same they're making bloody sure no one gets too close. Blokes being ghost-trained out every night to other prisons. Scared bloody rigid, they are. And so they should be—*bastards*. Here, Ron, what's up? Why you looking at me?'

'Where were you, Tony?'

'Eh?'

'You know what I mean.'

'Like hell I do.'

'All right then, have it your way. Be like that.'

'No, Ron, wait. Hang about. Okay, look, I'm sorry. But honest, it wasn't my fault.' He touched his friend's shoulder, tried in vain to meet his eyes. 'Here, did that copper go yakking to you?'

'No.'

'Well then . . .'

'He didn't need to, Tony, I *knew*.'

'How? How could you?'

''Cos I know *you*.'

They jogged in silence a while, faces lowered, out of step, out of sympathy . . . until at last Tony ran around in front to face him and try again. 'Listen, *please*. I want you to know . . .'

'Okay, Tony, okay.'

More jogging, rhythm starting to return now; yet it was a full circuit of the yard before they at last resumed their murmured exchanges.

'Ron, the word from the screws is that you did for Big Doyle.'

'That what they're saying, is it?'

'Yeah.' Rogers paused, waiting until they had passed the main group of supervision officers before: 'Not true, is it? I mean, if it was, they'd have you banged up safe in the seg unit.'

'Right, Tony, they would.' Briefly their eyes met. Hythe grinned and then shook his head at the absurdity of it. 'Can you honestly see me clobbering a big sod like him, eh?'

They guffawed, then both turned, checking as Hythe's name was called out by the duty SO. 'Hythe! Time's up!'

'Right, guv.'
'Who was it, Ron?'
'One of the Mufti, of course. Cheers, Tony.'
'Take care, old love.'
'I'll try, mate, I'll try.'

'She'll bring the tea directly.'
'Most welcome, Home Secretary.'
Roy Grantley pulled out his report and notes, anxious to get started. 'Number one, sir: the governor's managed to get all but six of the severely injured out of the Hammersmith and into the prison hospital. Secondly . . .'
'How badly injured are these six?'
'One skull fracture. The rest a combination of cracked ribs and damaged internal organs—liver, ruptured spleen. It's anticipated that a couple may become the subject of assault proceedings.'
'Against staff?'
'No, Home Secretary, prisoners. Those acutely injured were mostly either IRA or sex offenders. I do have full details for you here.'
He paused as the statuesque secretary brought in the tray of tea things, poured, smirked and left.
'Secondly, there's a preliminary report from the governor roundly condemning the wing governor, Pelham. Hanford blames him for the prior deterioration in inmate morale and staff discipline, then goes on to accuse him of worsening the consequences of the riot itself.'
'Oh dear.'
'He claims that Pelham was aware of his own responsibility for the outbreak of the riot and accordingly sought to play down its severity, regardless of the havoc that was going on. He says that but for Pelham's consistently misleading assessments, he would have sent the Mufti officers in at a much earlier stage, thus minimizing both the human injuries and suffering and the material damage to the wing.'

'Hm. All sounds rather messy.'

'I'm afraid so, Home Secretary. Moreover, he thinks that Pelham might well try to counter these accusations by talking to the press.'

'Be in breach of the Official Secrets Act if he does—for what that's worth these days.'

'Thirdly, sir, a complaint from the chairman of the Brentford Board of Visitors about Hanford. The Board feel he's being less than forthcoming about the riot: trying to withhold details of injuries and so forth.' Grantley cleared his throat, flicking biscuit crumbs from his jacket. 'Frankly, I agree with them. I quite welcomed the opportunity of rebuking Hanford.'

He paused to shuffle his papers to the final item.

'Fourthly, we've had representations from the Prison Officers' Association citing the riot as a direct consequence of all these criminal psychopaths they've got in A Wing. They've documented it all: the injuries, those allegedly responsible for assaults and violence, identities of ringleaders and so on.' .

Savage was nodding in approval, showing his first real sign of animation since they'd got the tea in. 'What sort of a case do you think they'll make of it?'

'Depends on how much they overstate it. For instance, they're trying to tie in this suspect Hythe. But according to the prison psychiatrist they're wrong to try and label Hythe as a psychopath. Clinically schizophrenic, yes; personality disorder, yes. But nowhere near the types they're now refusing to treat in Broadmoor.'

'None the less, Roy, you can expect his defence lawyers to trot out plenty of damning psychiatric evidence at a trial. Diminished responsibility and so on.'

'Ah, as to that, Home Secretary, I understand a full trial is now unlikely. Apparently there's a good prospect of his pleading guilty to manslaughter.'

*

Ronald Hythe was on his knees retrieving the more elusive
of Butch's feathers from the corner of his cell when he heard
a key thrust into the lock. He scrambled to his feet to face
the door as it opened. To his surprise, it was a landing officer
with a bucket of warm water, a squeezie and detergent.

'Reckoned you'd want to give the place a scrub out.'

'Hey, thanks, guv.'

The officer nodded, moving Hythe's chair across to the
doorway where he sat down to watch as the prisoner started
to wash down the walls of his cell.

'Anything you want, Ronnie, you just have to ask.'

'Yeah?' Hythe tried to hide the suspicion in his sidelong
glance. Never trust a screw: the golden rule; so what the
hell was this one up to?

'No sweat, Ronnie,' the man reassured him. 'After all,
you've earned yourself a spoiling.'

'Yeah?'

'You're the hero of the wing.' Then, at Hythe's continued
unease and confusion: 'Look, you made a score. You felled
that big Irish turd for us. And so far as me and the lads are
concerned, that wins you the medal. Man of the match,
know what I mean?'

'Oh.' Relief surged through Hythe, high and tingling like
a sniff of cocaine.

'Doyle had all of us after him. Not just 'cos he was Irish
but because he was waging his own personal campaign
against us. A patriotic duty, that's how he saw it. How else
do you suppose he got himself in and out the block all the
time? 'Cos he was always bristling up to us, that's why.'

'Yeah?' The slow grin on Ronnie Hythe's face preceded
the first laughter he'd managed in days. 'The bastard had
it coming to him, then.'

'And how.' The officer nodded. 'So don't you have no
fears for yourself. You're back among friends now, old lad.'

With which, as earnest to his promise, he searched in his
top pocket then leaned forward to toss a joint on to the bed.

'You enjoy a puff at that later on, courtesy of the lads. Okay?'

'Hey, ta, guv.'

'And another thing: don't you worry about the consequences. Any extra bird they give you, you're going to serve it in style. Guaranteed home comforts, good section reports, the lot.'

Hythe abandoned the cleaning and moved to sit on the bed. The relief of talking, even to a screw, was intense. 'My brief reckons he can get me a deal if I'll change my evidence. Sentence to run concurrent.'

'Oh yes? What's he saying you've got to change then?'

'Oh, well—' caution returned briefly—'just, you know, to do with what I can remember.'

'And what's that?'

'Well, like, details of the fight.'

'What details?'

'Well, you know, so long as I'll say the same as what Connolly and McGuire are saying, that'll be okay.'

'Yes, lad, yes, I can see that. And that could help you in other ways and all.'

'Yeah?'

The officer glanced at his watch, then stood up, hoisting the chair back into place. 'I'll leave you the bucket till later.'

'What other ways, guv?'

'Eh?' The man paused in the act of leaving. 'Well, just that anyone else involved is going to feel a lot happier to know that.'

'Er, sorry, guv, who? Who else do you mean?'

'No one special. But just supposing there *was* someone, he'd naturally want to make good and sure you're singing the same song as them other two, right?'

The clang of the massive cell door echoed explosively through Hythe's head. He sat rigidly still for a time. Finally he picked up the joint, stared blankly at it a moment and then, with a cry, flung it among the feathers in the corner.

*

'Lawrence, this is the governor of A Wing, Mr Ashley Pelham.'

The ITN editor gave him the full VIP routine, jumping up to shake hands, then fussing around with chairs and offers of refreshment before inquiring what had been agreed between them.

'Mr Pelham wants to discuss the legal side.'

'Legal?' The editor sat down rather abruptly.

'As an employee of the Prison Department, you see, I'm subject to the Official Secrets Act. Constrained from making any public statement without prior clearance.'

'Only in theory, Mr Pelham. Recent cases have shown the act to be far less binding than was originally thought.' Then, with a chuckle: 'You're not likely to find yourself facing charges of high treason.'

'Lawrence . . .'

'Sorry if that sounded flippant. But the fact is, about the worst that's likely to happen is that you'll be held in breach of contract and fired. Which, if you think you're for the chop anyway, becomes largely academic.'

There was a pause. Lawrence Cawley gestured in apology, aware that he wasn't hitting quite the right note.

'Er, did I get it wrong about the job?'

'Suppose we were to tape Mr Pelham's account of the riot and its origins. I've pointed out to him that in view of the impending inquiry, we can expect to have a court injunction slapped on us.'

'Not if we keep it secret before transmission.'

'Which we can't if we follow established right-of-reply practice.'

The editor sighed, rolled his bottom lip in disapproval but nodded reluctant acknowledgement. He knew now, because Kate Lewis had pulled this one before, what was coming, and he deeply disapproved. ITN's function, as he had pointed out to her the first time, was to provide a public service, not a private protection agency.

'So you're proposing we tape it, then edit and sit on it; so that Mr Pelham can then use its existence as a big stick to wave over the head of the Chief Inspector of Prisons, hm?' Pause. 'Most charitable towards you, Mr Pelham, but what does ITN get out of it—apart, that is, from a lot of ill-will from the Whitehall mandarins?'

Another pause. Finally the editor grunted in resignation, spreading his hands as though to forestall further argument.

'Very well, very well. It so happens that Tim is interviewing the Bishop of Durham at three-thirty. If you were to tack on to the end of that then God might know about it, but I wouldn't nor would Alistair Burnett nor, above all, would the controller. Goodbye, Mr Pelham. I hope for your sake we never get to screen your tape.'

Walsh found the door of DCS Mason's office ajar. He tapped and, forcing a grin, went in to face him. 'Got a moment, Dave?'

'Jack, old sport, I reckoned you'd come chasing around to see me sooner or later.'

Walsh knew nothing factual on his colleague, had little more than that uneasy feeling that Mason had slithered down the road down which he himself might so easily have slithered. Over the years he had seen Dave Mason develop an aura of slyness and guilt, living rather too lavishly for his copper's income: flash car, jazzy Med holidays, a taste for the casinos. No breach of regulations in any of that, of course; merely a betrayal of the unwritten code of conduct to which senior detectives were obliged to conform. It didn't much help that once, as wooden-tops together on the beat, he and Dave had been close mates.

Walsh pulled a chair across to beside the desk, sat down and waved aside the offer of a cigar.

'Taking retirement soon, I hear.'

'That's right.'

'You'd think young Blaize would have slipped you one with a few ex's for your sock.'

'I suggested the Cayman Islands, but he wouldn't buy it.'

Mason grinned, reaching into a drawer for a print-out on the original Hythe murder case.

'There wasn't a lot to it. Impulse killing. Took a carving knife to his wife. Cut her down in the kitchen while she was making coffee for a neighbour who was sat through in the living-room. According to Hythe, it was triggered by things she'd just been saying about him. Anyway, he behaved himself: didn't get stuck into the neighbour or anything; simply ran out of the house with the knife, straight along to the local station and gave himself up. Well, no, hang on, he did make a show of trying to knife himself at the station, but nothing the desk sergeant couldn't head off easy enough.'

He paused to light the cigar, absorbed with his recollec- tions as he puffed at it. 'Sad little geezer. He'd been catching a lot of stick—not just from this slag but all the rest: lost his job, got behind with the rent and HP and that. Also they'd lost a kid the year before. Whooping cough. He'd been hitting the booze. The shrinks reckoned it was the combination of that plus all the stress which had brought out his underlying schizoid bit. His brief trotted out all the usual at the trial about it being a cry for help, identity crisis, latent homosexuality, all that crut. Trying for a diminished responsibility manslaughter. Anyway, the jury didn't swallow it. Hardly surprising, given the carve-up job matey had done on her in the kitchen.'

Walsh gave a noncommittal grunt, glancing up from making notes. 'Any previous?'

'Nothing heavy. Petty thieving, t-&-d, bit of Borstal. But he'd grown out of it. Straight for ten years before this blew up.'

Mason gave him a wink as he slid the print-out across, then sat back to draw on the cigar and blow a plume of smoke. He sees himself as one of God's chosen, Walsh thought; poor misguided bastard: no less of a sad little geezer than Ronnie Hythe, if only he could but see it . . . the corrupted victim of an occupational disease.

'He's not a villain, Jack,' the man was saying. 'Not the sort we're used to dealing with. Of course, I can't say what a few years in the nick might have done to him. But the Ronald Hythe I charged with murder four years ago was just a straight little block who'd hit one wobbly too many and gone over the edge.'

There was a pause. Walsh folded the print-out and stood up. Mason glanced up at him in query. 'Is that what he's done this time? Gone over the edge?'

'Maybe.'

'Another knife job?'

'As it happens, no. No knife, no stress and as yet no confession.' Walsh moved to leave, conceding a wry nod in acknowledgement of the help. 'As usual, Dave, you had the easy one, I get the dog.'

'I heard you'd got more than that, Jack.'

'Like what?'

'Like someone asking around the office—someone sussing you out.' He snorted in reassurance, wagging his head at Walsh's abrupt frown. 'No prizes for ID'ing the interested party in a case stuck where yours is, mate.'

'Someone in the Prison Service?'

'We'll make a detective of you yet.'

CHAPTER 9

'Where are you heading us, Taff? This isn't the way to the prison.'

'No, guv'nor.' DI Roberts let a pause go by as he accelerated away from traffic lights and along the King's Road.

'Something I thought we should take a look at.'

'Well?' Pause. 'So don't play games. You know I want to get this case stitched up by tonight.'

Roberts slowed the car, turning to eye his chief.

'We both do, guv. But it's just not coming together like that, is it?'

'Like what? Don't talk in riddles.'

'Well, for a start, the forensic evidence doesn't tie it in with Hythe.'

'Doesn't eliminate him either.'

'No, but . . .'

'Suppose we wait until we hear what he's going to tell us later on. Now where the hell are you taking me?'

'To watch a video tape. It won't take long.'

'Where? Your place?'

'Matter of fact, no. This bird—the fancy piece I was with last night—her place.'

'So she's not just something you latched on to in the pub?'

Taff grinned in evasion and cleared his throat. In point of fact, when Kate had suggested it the previous evening, he hadn't held out much hope of getting Walsh along to hear the tape.

Diawl, the very thought of Walsh agreeing to an informal liaison with the press! But then, as the day had worn on and they'd run up against all this dodgy nonsense over Hythe, the DI had got into one of his rare moments of revolt: stand up and speak out, boyo, and to hell with the consequences . . . Not that there'd be any if Kate had been held up and failed to get home in time to greet them.

Her name was there, of course, on a neatly-inscribed card above the bellpush. Taff did his best to conceal it as he rang, but Walsh was too sharp for him.

'Kate bloody Lewis!'

'Listen, guv—'

'Have you taken leave of your senses?'

'Straight up, guv'nor, she's okay. No sweat.'

Walsh turned, going to push past him towards the car.
The DI stepped back to head him off, simultaneously
beckoning to Kate as she appeared in the doorway.

'At least see the tape now we're here. There's no one
going to know.'

'You're familiar with Force orders re informal contacts
with the press . . .'

'Yeah—sure—okay. But we also have a duty to get at all
the facts of a case.'

Walsh paused, pulling a face, conscious by now of Kate's
presence and also of his DI's uncharacteristic flush of revolt.
Abruptly he swung to face the reporter, his expression taut
with reproach.

'You realize, Miss Lewis, what a conspiracy like this
could cost DI Roberts?'

'Conspiracy? Two people meet in a pub . . .'

'*Not* by chance. Don't try and bullshit me, miss.'

It was with some difficulty that Kate stood her ground.
From that first brief glimpse of Walsh outside the prison on
the evening of the riot, Kate had placed him as the sort of
copper which experience had led her to distrust: a senior
detective of the old school, stubborn, inflexible and chauvinistic; averse to the media to an almost paranoid degree; a
man whose substantial power had led to arrogance and even
a measure of disdain for the law; a man who, while not
actively corrupt, had let expediency corrode his integrity.

And yet there it was: the *de facto* situation. Sup with the
devil, Miss Bright-Eyes, for there is no way into this story
other than through him with the mask of deceit and the
tufted eyebrows.

Beside them, Roberts-the-Welsh was fidgeting, aware of
the curiosity of passers-by—of strangers who would likely
recognize Kate and even, conceivably, his chief from the
TV pictures after the riot.

'Come on, guv, no one's going to be compromised by a

quick dekko at a tape. Think of Miss Lewis just as an informant offering help. Come on.'

Walsh muttered something under his breath; but then, to their huge relief, he gestured in resignation, swung round and headed for the entrance.

Kate's flat came as a surprise to Taff. Somehow, shaped perhaps by lingering perceptions of the TV celebrity, he had expected to find the split-level, open-plan luxury beloved of studio set designers. Instead he found himself in a routine, none-too-tidy, two-bedroom apartment of the type rented out fully-furnished and functional to those with the means to pay but neither the time nor inclination to make improvements.

'Excuse the mess,' Kate remarked, ushering them in. 'I only just managed to get back from recording an interview.' She waved a video cassette at them. 'I've brought the tape of that as well. It's with the assistant governor in charge of A Wing.'

'You bloody idiot, Taff.'

'Nothing to do with me, guv. Honest.'

'Like hell it isn't!' Walsh jerked angrily round to confront the two of them. 'Let's get this totally clear from the start: whatever you two have got going together, it is now terminated for the duration of this case, understood? Miss Lewis, neither I nor my DI have any form of liaison going with you or your company. If you've got hold of information which you believe could assist us in our investigation, fair enough, hand it over. But don't expect any form of *quid pro quo* in return. Got it?'

'Received and understood.' She resisted the impulse to salute. Glancing at Taff, she found that he was staring intently at the ceiling but otherwise showed no sign of remorse. 'I'll run you the tape of the prisoner's wife first. Did Mr Roberts explain anything about it to you?'

'He can do that later.' Walsh cleared his throat, glaring at Taff. 'Along with the other explaining he's got to do.'

'If you mean about how we met . . .'

'Just run the tape, Miss Lewis. We're in a hurry.'

It was a drastic move for Kate to take. Normally, to preview ITN tapes to any outsider, let alone to coppers, would have been unthinkable. But in this instance—anxious to trade into a liaison with the murder squad on the case, and with neither tape anyway scheduled for screening— Kate had reckoned it a worthwhile gamble: precious little to lose by it, and potentially rewarding if it won her an in with Big Chief Walsh.

The senior detective made a point of keeping his overcoat on, however, and remained standing throughout the play- back of the interview. After it, he made no comment other than to grunt assent when she offered to run the Pelham tape as well. This, too, he watched through in silence to the end, then gave a grunt as she switched off the set.

'That it, then?' He registered her nod, then turned to- wards the door, jerking his head for Taff to follow. 'Don't know why you should imagine that lot's going to help us.'

'Purely as background, Mr Walsh.' Then, as he opened the door: 'The way I heard it, you're one of the Yard's more thorough men. No stone unturned and all that. Since the A Wing riot gave rise to Doyle's death, I assumed information on the background to that riot might be of value to you. If I was wrong, I apologize for wasting your time.'

Walsh had paused, his expression cold and unyielding. Now he gestured for his DI to go on ahead and, starting to pull the door shut behind them, added curtly: 'Chances are we'll be charging a man very shortly, Miss Lewis. In that event you may expect us to hold a short press conference at the Yard. Very short, if I have my way. Good day to you.'

'John Tanner speaking, Mr Smith. I got a message you were trying to reach me.'

'That's right. I said I'd keep in touch. Well, the latest is that Kate Lewis taped an interview with the governor of A

Wing this afternoon. I was watching up in the gallery and I can tell you he was extremely forthcoming about the riot.'

'Oh cripes . . .'

'Most outspoken about contributory actions by the wing staff. Seen in conjunction with the other interview—the one I told you she taped with the prisoner's wife—it all adds up to quite an indictment.'

'The damned fool.'

'Although his main target was the prison governor, there's a strong implication that Hanford's actions—and omissions —were prompted out of sympathy with your people. The thrust of it is that Hanford is not his own master—that he's so paranoid about industrial action he's been yielding to POA pressure for months.'

'Mr Smith . . .'

'Steve, please.'

'Okay, Steve, thanks. Listen, I don't know how Miss Lewis got hold of our Mr Ashley Pelham, but there's a lot you ought to know about him before screening that tape: like, for instance, that his days are definitely numbered with the Prison Service and he knows it. Like, for instance, there's recently been several complaints lodged against him by this branch re the laxness of discipline on A Wing. Like, he's going to catch a lot of criticism in the forthcoming inquiry into the A Wing riot—which last point is damn-sure the reason he's gone blabbing to ITN.'

'Well, there you go, John: ample grounds for either you or Hanford to get a court injunction to stop transmission.'

'You reckon?'

'I've already warned the editor to expect a block on it.'

'Good on you.'

'It's in a good cause, brother. Now how about things your end? You got anything for me?'

'As it happens, yes. Something I just picked up from one of our lads on A Wing. The man Hythe—the prisoner I told you about—he's decided to come clean: pleading guilty to manslaughter.'

'Lawrence, old jug, I just picked up a whisper on the Doyle killing. The word is that the CID officers on the case are reckoning to charge someone very shortly. Could even be a press conference at the Yard this evening.'

'Yes, Kate, yes, that fits.'

'Oh? With what?'

'Steve was just on to his union contact. The man they're going to charge will be that prisoner, Ronald Hythe. Apparently he's decided to plead to manslaughter.'

Kate frowned, half recalling something Taff Roberts had said the previous evening or else had implied when he talked about closed doors and lack of cooperation—whichever, she had the feeling of something inconsistent, something amiss.

'So anyway, it could all be stitched up by tonight.'

'I hope so, Kate. I want you at the Old Bailey tomorrow to cover the Hell's Angels case.'

While they were waiting for Hythe to be escorted across to the incident room, Walsh rang through to his wife. She sounded a shade defensive.

'Jack, I've confirmed for the Met Benevolent Association bash tomorrow night. Eight o'clock at the Savoy, all right?'

'Assuming it all works out this end, fine.'

'Alison Blaize says there's no doubt of it.'

'What the bloody hell does Alison Blaize know about it?'

'Presumably what her husband's told her. I don't know, Jack. She just said to me: Oh, that Brentford thing's all over and done with.'

'Fantastic.'

'Well, isn't it over?'

'Chummy's on his way over right now. Give it another half-hour and we may be privileged to know what Alison Blaize knows.'

'I see.'

'I wish I did.'

'Well, listen, you be sure and get it done with. I've got a lovely roast ready for this evening.'

'I'll try.'

'Bring Taff with you. Tell him Heather's cooking it special for him.'

'Here, she's not, is she?'

'Don't worry. Just be sure and get here.'

'Ronald Hythe, you are not obliged to say anything unless you wish to do so, but what you do say may be put into writing and given in evidence. Okay? Now then, you had a talk with your solicitor?'

'I did, chief, yes.'

There was a pause, expectant on the one side, cautious and uncertain on the other. Hythe's hand rose unconsciously to finger the area of bruising at the back of his head: the wound which, almost like a reproach, lingered as a physical reminder of the truth which everyone seemed intent on his renouncing.

'He—er—Mr Spink gave me to understand I could expect a deal.'

'Oh? Who with?'

'Well, er, like, I suppose, with the Law, know what I mean?'

'No idea, Mr Hythe.' Walsh swung round to his DI. 'You any notion what Mr Spink could have meant, Inspector?'

'None, sir. Not unless it was something to do with Mr Hythe copping a guilty plea.'

'Yeah, guv, yeah, that's right. That's what he said to me. Forget all that about being thumped by the officer; don't risk no jury trial; just plead to manslaughter and that'll go easy on you.'

Walsh let a longish pause go by before rapping the words out at him. 'That it, then? That what you're doing?'

Another pause, Hythe once again fingering the wound. Then at last, his voice down almost to a pleading whine: 'I suppose that's down to you, guv.'

'How'd you figure that?'

'You tell me, guv. You tell me what to say.' Then, in a rush: 'It ain't no good me going against what you want. You're the boss. It's just that I keep remembering how, the other night in the hospital, you said you wasn't taking sides; you said all you cared about was the *facts*. Right?'

Ron Hythe paused, hoping for some confirmation but got only a bleak stare. 'Well, I'm sorry, guv, but that's what I told you before: the facts. About that officer giving me this clump round the back of me noddle. But, like, it's down to you whether or not I'm going to *say* that in my statement. You just give me the nod and, fair enough, I'll forget the facts and go for the fiction, know what I mean.'

In the ensuing silence, Taff saw the anguish draw at his chief's face before he looked away, fumbling impulsively in his jacket for the fags he no longer carried.

Earlier, on the drive from Kate's flat, he had remained austerely silent, delaying the rebuke which Taff had known must come. Only in the last stretch, as they had waited at the Kew Bridge junction, had he demanded to know why on earth his DI had risked such a damn-fool breach of regulations with the press. Surprisingly, he had not risen to Taff's defiant retort that, to hell, if he couldn't trust in his DI's discretion after all the jobs they'd worked on together, well too damn bad!

It struck him now as a bizarre irony that this grotty, sly-eyed little lifer sitting across the desk had so neatly if unwittingly punted the ball back into Walsh's end of the pitch.

Taff got up, moving to fill the coffee percolator as a diversion to ease the tension, bracing himself for the curt gruffness of his chief's likely reply that, since lawyers knew what was best for their clients, Mr Hythe had better go along with what Mr Spink advised. That was the system, after all: the way things were done. It wasn't for him, much less his DI, to go rocking the boat or looking for ideal solutions in an imperfect world.

But no such reply came. Indeed, to Taff's surprise, on turning from the percolator, he saw Walsh's teeth were bared in a grin, if not with pleasure certainly with resolve.

'Inspector Roberts and I—' he had to pause to clear his throat—'we weren't called into this nick to bend things, lad. You stay with the facts, like you remember them. You get it all written down—how you were fighting with Doyle, how he pushed you back and you were then knocked out cold by the Mufti officer—then you can go over it with Mr Spink, get him to witness your signature and then give it to us.'

'Yeah?' Hythe's obvious surprise was tinged, ironically enough, with suspicion. 'And then what?'

'Naturally, we shall continue our efforts—first to confirm the presence of that officer and then to identify him.'

'But, guv, supposing you can't?' The whole ethos of lies and deceit so basic to 'nick culture' surged in the prisoner, his expression reflecting the very duplicity he now feared. 'I mean, you know what it's like in here. No one's going to talk. No one. Not them Irish gits and certainly not the screws. So . . .'

'So you just get on with your statement.' Walsh rummaged in a drawer for some SY-9 forms and a caution card, then slid them across the desk. 'Write it all out on these witness forms. Start it off with: *I make this statement of my own free will* then copy out the words on this card from where it says *I have been cautioned that anything I say* . . . Okay? Then follow all that with your statement of facts. Then just leave us to sort out the rest.'

'All very well to say that, guv, when you're not in the line of fire like me.'

''Maybe we're not.' Walsh's glance flicked ruefully at his DI. 'But be sure we're not exactly in raptures either.'

'Tomorrow morning at the earliest, Chief Superintendent.'

'Miss Horn, it's very urgent.'

'I'm afraid the governor went off home early to work on his report. Sorry.'

'How early tomorrow?'

'I could try and fit you in before adjudications at nine.'

'I'll be with you at eight-fifty.'

Walsh groaned as he rang off, then pointed accusingly at his DI. 'And damn you, Taff Roberts.'

'Me, guv'nor? What did I do?'

'You know bloody well! Sitting there like Banquo's ghost, pushing me to buck the system. For heaven's sake, we're behaving like a couple of wooden-tops. Everyone telling us to let the ruddy lifer carry it and stop trying to be so bloody smart. And all we do is tell him to stick to his original version—which is probably all lies anyway—while we try and trace this Mufti thug who like as not never existed!'

There was a pause as Taff poured them coffee, hoping his chief would leave it at that. He didn't.

'We're not in the business of do-gooding. That's not the road to promotion and honourable retirement.'

'No, guv'nor.' Clearly this was but the edge of the storm, the forerunner to a tempest. The DI turned to reach for the telephone. 'I'll try Mr Pelham, see if he can help us with those Mufti names.'

'Fat hope of that.'

Nor was there. The A Wing duty SO connected Taff through to Pelham's deputy who said that the wing governor was unavailable. Pressed for details, he revealed that Ashley Pelham had been suspended from further duties and sent home about an hour earlier; as to the reason for this suspension, however, he professed total ignorance.

Walsh scowled, drumming his fingers. 'It'll be your Kate

Lewis—that damn-fool recording she got him to tape.'

'Word got back pretty sharpish if that is the reason.'

'That's the system again, boyo. Pelham takes on the Establishment and, wham, he's in it over his ears before he knows what's hit him.' Walsh heaved up out of his chair, pointing in reproach at his DI as he moved round from behind his desk. 'Same as you'll be in it if you go playing clever buggers with the press again.' He shrugged into his overcoat, then tossed Taff his anorak. 'Come on. Everyone else is off home, so we might as well do the same. Dell said she's got a roast on the go for us.'

'Er—sorry, guv'nor.'

'What do you mean? You're invited for a meal . . .'

Taff pulled on the anorak and followed the chief out. He locked the office, hurried after him along the corridor and down the stairs, waiting until they were outside in the fresh night air before repeating the apology.

'It's going to be best if I don't come, guv'nor.'

'Rubbish. Heather's home. We'll pick up some wine, relax, have some laughs.'

'Except we won't, will we.' Then, overriding the senior officer's retort: 'Sorry, but it's always the same: have a few drinks, start talking about the case, start going over it, detail by dreary detail; Dell and Heather get fed up; you and I get more and more chocker and pig-headed. We end up yelling at each other . . . Sorry, guv'nor, but we're best giving it a miss.'

Walsh took it in silence, waiting until they were in the car before retaliating. Tired and demoralized though he was, he knew his DI was right. The curse of the investigator: the mind too focused on the challenge to let go. With or without Taff there, with or without booze, he knew it would be the same: the facts, the evidence, the contradictions, the suspicions, the possibilities, the alternatives; all going round and round in his mind, jumbling and churning like the ingredients in a pudding mix . . . the nightmare cost of

obsession, the penalty of passion . . . And all of it yet another
variation of that same occupational disease.

'You're bullshitting me, boy. You're just reckoning to
chase off after that Lewis tart.'

'Even if I was, guv'nor, that's no business of yours.'

'It bloody is! In breach of standing orders, it is!'

'You'll need proof if you're going to report me.'

Kate Lewis was not the domesticated type, any more for
that matter than was the inner Kathy. Had she been so,
Kathy might have rejected the prospect of Kate and instead
stayed married, had kids and rejoiced in family. Instead the
journalist in her had applied for the screen job, had got and
rejoiced in that, saddened only by the probable consequences for her marriage. Bill was a nice guy and she
regretted their divorce; they still met from time to time,
doing so without animosity, both accepting that their priori-
ties and expectations had tuned out to be incompatible.

None the less, with help from *Dallas*, she was diligently
attacking a mound of ironing that evening when the doorbell
went and, going through to answer it, she found herself
smiling at the man of the Valleys.

'Fancy coming out for a meal?'

'Sorry, but I'm on call for a late press conference at
Scotland Yard. A man's due to be charged on the A Wing
killing.'

'Ah.' Taff revealed the bottle of Goldener Oktober he was
holding. 'Then I'd better come in.'

She found him a corkscrew, then killed J.R. and started
to tidy away the ironing.

'Don't let the domestic scene fool you: I'm basically just
a good-timer. What happened to the press conference?'

Taff finished uncorking, poured the wine, gave her a glass
and drank their mutual health before replying. 'The answer
to that one, oddly enough, seems to be *you*.' With which,
ignoring her surprise, he moved her across to the settee,

shared another toast and then a very warm, suggestive kiss before attempting the explanation.

'The chain of responsibility goes like this: You to Harry, Harry to me, me to that mad answering phone of yours, you and I to the Bag o' Nails. Okay so far?'

'Smashing.'

'Now then, such is your dynamic influence that, for all my years of hardened CID cynicism, I suddenly burst out in a rash of conscience.'

'Not contagious, I hope.'

'Well, gal, that's just it: because I got uppity with old Jack Walsh, we ended up this afternoon with him stood over there watching those tapes. But then it went further. He knew I was all for bucking the system; so when it came to the crunch at the prison, he knew he wouldn't be able to look either me or his better self in the eye unless—well, never mind the unlesses. The end result of it is no one charged and no press conference.'

'Ronald Hythe not pleading to manslaughter after all, eh?'

'Bloody hell, woman, you're not supposed to know that much!'

'Sorry.'

'Mind you, Sod's Law as usual, Jack Walsh and I seem to be the last to know every damn thing on this jinxy old case.' He gave a groan in wry echo of his chief. 'Right now the poor old devil's drinking himself silly and demanding to know how he committed such a sacrilege.'

Taff paused to lean forward and repeat the kiss. 'So there, you see, it all comes back to you.'

'It's just another case, Dell. That's what I keep telling myself. No point getting my knickers in a twist over it. All part of the day's work—part of the job.'

Dell Walsh muttered something sympathetic, kept her head down over the dress she was altering for the Savoy do and regretted yet again the absence of Taff Roberts. What else were blessed DIs for, after all, if not to act as the butt for their governors' gripes? Not that Dell herself was unused to such outbursts: increasingly over the last few years, whenever a sticky case came along, first the bottle, then the worries. Well, roll on retirement!

And yet, for all the familiar symptoms—the fretting and repetition, over and over—tonight there was a difference: a deeper frustration perhaps, and yet a sense, if not of actual excitement, certainly of obstinacy.

For Ronald Hythe that night, bereft of such palliatives as whisky and wife, the anxieties were sharper by far. Insomnia, although less of a problem since Grendon, had now returned with a vengeance, the more so tonight because now when he moved his head he not only felt the pain of the bruise but also heard the crinkle of the papers concealed in his pillow-case.

He had laboured throughout the evening over the composition of his statement, refining and perfecting it, burning to ash the several false starts he'd made and then stowing the finished version inside the pillow-case. While it would not be safe in there in the event of a systematic cell spin by the landing staff, it was a fair precaution at least against less formal intrusion.

Time and again he recalled the subtle menace behind the landing officer's words that afternoon: . . . *supposing there was someone, he'd naturally want to make good and sure you're singing the same song as them other two* . . . which, stupid, bum-brained twat that he was, he had now decided against! Decided, moreover, on the advice of a ruddy copper, for Christ's sake!

The night dragged wretchedly on, tainted with fears, punctuated with the crinkling of the paper . . . until, somewhere in the small hours, it escalated into terror as, rolling over he registered the dim light up near the top of the door where the peephole cover had been silently swivelled aside. He lay dead still, watching it in dread, waiting for the stealthy turning of a key in the door ... until, after an eternity, he managed to slide out of bed, creep to the door and peer cautiously out.

No one there: no watching eye or lurking shadow. Just the pinhole view across the void to Cell 40 on the opposite side. Slowly, trembling despite the warmth in the overheated cell, the lifer crept back to lie on his bed, his gaze fixed hypnotically on the sinister beam of light ... which, when the clanging and shouts started for slop-out at eight the next morning, he found had at some time been covered once again as stealthily as it had been opened.

DAY FOUR

CHAPTER 10

'Now then, Chief Superintendent, just what's so urgent?'

Hanford's manner, although brisk, was noticeably less hostile. Indeed, there was the impression almost of satisfaction in his manner as, half rising, he gestured Walsh to one of the upright chairs opposite the elaborately carved oak desk.

'I want to conclude this case and get off your patch soon as possible, Governor, that's what.'

'I understood you'd as good as tied it up already.'

'Really, sir?'

'Got your confession from Ronald Hythe, at least.'

'I see.' Walsh's face masked a reciprocal satisfaction that at least the smug bugger didn't know everything. 'What I want from you, sir, priority, is the names of those Mufti officers most likely to have been first up to the Fours landing during the terminal phase of the riot.'

The effect was galvanic, Hanford rising to swing abruptly away and face out of the double windows behind his desk.

'Why?'

'Privilege of the investigating officer . . .'

'Don't come that with me!' The governor swung back to lean his knuckles on the desk, the hostility hard and blatant now. 'Those officers were responsible to *me*. If you want to question them, you'll have to have a damn good reason.'

'A man murdered . . .'

'You've got a self-defence manslaughter plea. That's enough!'

'Whether I have or not, I still want those names . . .'

'What do you think you're playing at, man? Got some sort of hang-up, have you? Some sort of power complex? Reckoning to pull rank, throw your weight around? Well, let me remind you that my authority in this prison far exceeds yours!'

He was sweating, Walsh noticed, a nervous tic pulling beside one of the pouchy eyes.

'The names, Governor. I understand the assault was spearheaded by a section code-named the Blacks—a section consisting of eighteen officers drawn, as it happens, from this prison.'

'I had no option, damn it! We were short of men—especially officers familiar with the lay-out in that wing.'

'I'm not questioning your decision to use local officers, sir. Merely asking for their names.' He stood up, moving to leave, aware that there was no chance of getting anything here and now, deciding to avoid too implacable a refusal from which it would be that much harder for Hanford to back down later. 'I'd appreciate your earliest possible response.'

DI Roberts was humming *Land of my Fathers* as he located the Pelhams' semi and went up the garden path to knock on the door. His choice of patriotic music was significant, there being an element of bravado in his presence at the Pelhams' place; for, with a chief like Jack Walsh, you went out on a limb at your peril.

The freckle-faced Scotswoman who opened the door was visibly tense. The detective put on a reassuring smile, presented his warrant card and asked to see her husband. Fiona Pelham made an effort, but already the resolve she had mustered before answering his knock was failing. To Taff's relief, however, Ashley Pelham appeared behind her in his dressing-gown.

'Please come in.' His smile held a hint of apology as he moved to grip his wife's shoulders. 'How about finding us some tea, love?' Then, nodding Taff through to the sitting-room: 'You'll have a cup, Inspector?'

'Never say no to that.'

'It's ironic,' Pelham said quietly as he closed the sitting-room door behind them. 'For ages now, Fiona's been on at me to get out. She's seen how out of kilter I've been with the job—at loggerheads with that oaf Hanford, in contention with his POA puppet-masters. But now it's actually come to it, she's in a fearful state about the future.'

He grimaced, wagging his head. 'Where does a prison governor find work, after all, other than in a prison?'

'You're experienced with people, sir. The bad, the mad and the sad. I'd think there'd be a good career for you in social work.'

Pelham shrugged, shaking his head. 'Except, as she shrewdly pointed out, they're also civil servants. Once you've messed in the Home Office nest, you know, selection boards can prove woefully bigoted.'

'Suspension isn't exactly the sack, sir.'

'You want a bet?' Then, gesturing in abrupt dismissal: 'Anyway, sorry to run on about me. How can I help?'

'It's about this claim of Hythe's to have been knocked unconscious by a Mufti officer. We're hoping to get some names.' Taff paused, registering the man's surprise. 'Something wrong, sir?'

'Simply that yesterday afternoon before I was suspended, the buzz around the wing staff was that Hythe's solicitor had jacked up a deal for him to plead to manslaughter.' He guffawed to hide his embarrassment. 'I must admit, when I heard about it, I was just a shade cynical about you and your chief.'

'Doing a deal, sir? It happens all the time.'

'I suppose so. But this time?'

'Not yet, so far as I know.'

'Uh-huh.' Pelham nodded in apparent relief. 'I can't say I *like* Ronnie Hythe. Sly and sycophantic. But I suppose the real issue here is the risk that a guilty officer might escape justice.'

He paused as his wife came in with the tray of tea-things, hurrying to clear a coffee-table of toys and then hand Taff the cup she poured him.

'One thing,' he resumed, 'I'm foxed to know how you're ever going to identify which of the Mufti officers it was.'

'The prison staff haven't exactly been falling over themselves to cooperate.'

'That hardly surprises you, surely.' Pelham sighed, pressing his hands flat together in thought. 'As I told you before, the group first up to the Fours was the contingent of local officers chosen to spearhead the assault because of their familiarity with the place. There were eighteen in all, but as to their identities, I can only put names to the half-dozen A Wing men.'

Taff had his notebook out in readiness. 'It's a start.'

'Let's see, then. Alf Harker, Jones, Green, McCann. Also the two you interviewed about the stretcher incident, Kedge and Binton.'

DI Roberts arrived at the incident room to find his chief having another session with Dominic Connolly. The Irish-

man was hunched tensely in his chair, hands gripped tight
to keep from shaking, eyes closed as if to exclude the superintendent's remorseless gaze. Yet, when he spoke, Walsh's
voice was low and calm with no hint of accusation.

'Go off and have a think about it, Mr Connolly. Off back
to your cell and . . .'

'Nothing to think about, sir.'

'That's a straight promise about the Maze prison. Obviously you'd be among much healthier company over there
—among fellow IRA men who'd see after you and act as a
block to the sort of reprisals you're likely to face here.'

Walsh sat back, eyeing Connolly and then turning to his
DI, head tilted for confirmation. 'That's right, isn't it,
Inspector Roberts? It was when he heard we could guarantee
him a transfer to the Maze that Kevin McGuire came clean
and told us about the Mufti officer attacking Doyle.'

Taff was aware of Connolly's gaze jerking round at him,
probing for veracity or deceit.

'That's what did it, chief, yes: the safety of getting to the
Maze.'

'You taped him before,' Connolly piped up, 'how come
you haven't got no tape of him saying about that?'

'Obviously, he made us stop taping it. He said he wasn't
going to risk having *anything*, not on tape nor written out,
which could expose him in advance of the court proceedings.'

Connolly frowned, his mouth working in mute dispute;
but Walsh headed off further comment, spreading his hands
in benign reassurance, nodding for Taff to call in the escort
officer from outside.

'Think it over,' he repeated as the prisoner was led out.
'We'll have another talk later.'

Walsh waited until the door closed behind them, then
turned abruptly to his DI. 'Oversleep, did you?'

'No, guv'nor,' Taff indicated the list from Pelham but
held on to it as he asked: 'Any luck with Mr Hanford?'

'Names to follow. Why? What you got hold of there?' Taff handed over the list and explained its origin. 'Want to begin with Binton?'

Walsh stared at him in reproach, shaking his head. 'You're a chancer, boy.'

'I recall you saying that's a quality no CID lad should be without.'

'Oh? When?'

'Usually about your fifth Scotch, guv'nor.' He grinned, lifting the telephone. 'Binton?'

Walsh grunted affirmative, then pointed in renewed reproach. 'Got you all bright-eyed and bushy-tailed, hasn't she? Well, I hope to God in heaven you don't let her con you along, that's all!'

To Taff's relief a sharp rap on the door saved him from having to flannel out an answer. He gestured in apology and, nipping across to open up, found a rather flushed Geoffrey Spink brandishing a couple of sheets of handwritten paper.

'Hythe's statement.' He moved into the office and thrust it at Walsh to scan through. 'Notwithstanding the grammar, spelling and syntax, I imagine it will be to your satisfaction!'

The chief grunted, passing it to Taff to read as he eyed the angry solicitor. 'Only, sir, in so far as it conforms with Hythe's recollections of the incident.'

'He said that, in effect, you told him no deal.'

'Really, sir?' Walsh glanced at his DI. 'Is that how you recall it, Inspector?'

'Certainly not.' Then, to the solicitor: 'Mr Hythe asked us if he should put down the facts or the fiction, and that's . . .'

'I understand all too well what you're up to,' Spink cut in, resuming to Walsh. 'And I'm bound to say I regard it as petty and vindictive.'

'Really, sir? A rudimentary desire to get at the facts?'

'The *facts* are that Ronald Hythe is a convicted murderer

who is most probably lying about being hit over the head by this as yet unidentified officer. Whether he's lying or not, it's also a fact that no jury is likely to believe him about that. And it's a further, singularly distasteful fact that, by advising him to stick to this improbable story, you've contrived a situation where he can now be charged with murder rather than manslaughter—a charge which, given this statement, could well lead to a conviction: all the glory of a full-blown murder trial at the Bailey, you at the centre of the prosecution and reaping a rich harvest of professional status as a result!'

Taff Roberts, close to boiling over, was surprised to see his chief manage a bleak grin as he moved across to open the office door for the solicitor to leave.

'It's also a fact,' he remarked laconically, 'that if your client *is* charged with murder, he can retract this statement and revise his plea. Good day.'

'The prosecution will still use it against him.'

'Good day, sir.'

Taff managed to contain himself until Spink was actually out and the door closed before he let rip. 'You thinking what I'm thinking about that one, guv'nor?'

'Just another lawyer doing his job.'

'His job plus a few favours, I'd say.'

'For whom?'

'I reckon he's got chums in high places who've been leaning on him.'

'Yes?' Walsh was expressionless. 'Like who?'

'People who want Hythe to carry the can so that we'll stop asking questions.'

'You know what, Taff?' Walsh shook his head and winked. 'You're letting this case spook you. You're getting what the DACC likes to call paranoid perceptions.'

'A cover-up, Lawrence, that's what's going on!'

'If you say so, Sister Anna.'

'Don't patronize me!'

Kate moved closer out of earshot of the others seated around the big circular desk which filled the heart of ITN's newsroom. It had given her much satisfaction earlier that morning to be able to return from the Old Bailey with the news that, following representations from all three defence counsels, the Hell's Angels trial had been adjourned for yet a further week. The editor's response, however, had been prompt and disconcerting: very well then, off up to Birmingham with you to cover the latest Paki drugs bust. Kate, forced by this on to the offensive, had launched in about a cover-up at Brentford Prison involving the POA, the Prison Departent, doubtless the Cabinet as well. Although cover-up was a term which hard experience had taught her not to overdo, with this one she had little alternative and even fewer doubts.

'They've suspended Ashley Pelham; and there's a definite anti-leak hush-up operating in Whitehall; and—well, the Yard men on the case are getting high-level pressure to charge this prisoner, Hythe, and wrap up their investigation.'

Lawrence Cawley paused midway through unwrapping the day's first mini-cigar. 'Say again?'

'Hm?'

'About the police. How do you know that?'

'Well—er . . .'

'Come on.'

'Well, it stands to reason. I mean, look at the rumour Steve Smith picked up . . .'

'Kate, my sweet, for a seasoned reporter, you're an amazingly inept liar.'

'Bollocks!' She snatched the cigar and, ignoring his yell, lit and puffed angrily at it. 'Listen, this is *totally* secret. You promise that!'

'You've got an in with these detectives? Was that how you got on to Pelham?'

'It's how I know there's a cover-up and that what's going on is far too hot for you to exile me to frozen Birmingham on a no-no drugs thing.'

'All right, then. Just for the moment. But remember, I have budget allocations to worry about. I'm answerable to accountants and—'

'Yes, okay.' She was heading for the door. '*Secret!*'

'We've had to call you in, Mr Binton, for just a few more questions.'

'Sir.'

The officer presented as before: smart and erect, the military crispness there in his movements and tone.

'You'll be relieved to hear that the post-mortem findings by the Home Office pathologist confirmed what you'd been told before—that the injuries from Doyle's fall off the stretcher occurred *after* his death.' Walsh bared his teeth in a grin. 'If you did kill Patrick Doyle, it wasn't by dropping him down to the Threes.'

'Don't follow you, sir.'

'You haven't heard?' Walsh glanced briefly at his DI before resuming to Binton. 'We're now investigating the probability that one of the Mufti officers was responsible for Doyle's death.'

'I had no idea of that, sir.'

'Grapevine dried up for once?'

'Last rumour I heard, sir, had it that the prisoner Ronald Hythe was admitting to the crime.'

'Was that from a member of staff or . . .'

'Staff, sir. Never listen to a word from the cons. Mendacious lot.'

'Murderous lot as well. I acknowledge that, Officer. However, in this instance, as I said, we now have evidence incriminating a Mufti man in the killing.'

'May I ask what evidence, sir?'

'You may, yes. What I'd like from you is precise details

of how you led the Blacks up to the top landing.'

'Me, sir?' Binton went through his breathing ritual: draw down into deep lung, up on toes, rock back on to heels . . .

Their decision to summon Binton first had been prompted by Taff's interview impression of Kedge as a big thickie with neither the wit nor the imagination to lie convincingly; hence the logic of springing the surprise on smart-arse Binton, late of HM Armed Forces.

'Are you denying your participation in the Mufti group code-named the Blacks?'

'No, sir. Merely the implication that I was leading them.'

'Who was?'

'Principal Officer Harker, sir.'

'None the less, you were physically in the lead, were you not, during the struggle up the last flight of stairs?'

'May I ask who told you that, sir?'

Walsh shook his head, his teeth bared again in the grin. 'It's all right, Mr Binton, you're not under caution—merely preliminary questioning to test out uncorroborated evidence.' Another grin before: 'Be premature to start whistling up lawyers or union representatives.'

The officer took a pause for breath before rapping out his response. 'I am familiar with interrogation procedures, sir.'

'Ah. From your army days, of course.'

'In some measure.'

'In the Redcaps, were you?'

'No, sir.'

'None the less, that's why you were up there in the front of things—due to your military experience, hm? Expertise in close-combat work and so on.'

'Doesn't follow, sir. All officers have training in close-combat action.'

'None the less, having seen active service in, say, Northern Ireland, you'd be among the more confident and experienced.'

'Conceivably, sir.'

'Hence your presence in the thick of it—at the sharp end, so to speak.'

'To the best of my recollection, I may have been among the first half-dozen or so up to the Fours.'

'Ah.'

'I certainly wasn't in the lead. Nor was there by then all that much resistance. The toughest part, to my recollection, was gaining access to the Twos, what with both stairways, south and north, being barricaded with cell furniture, lockers and so on. We were obliged to send in a mole man with a big hook, sheltering him on either side with our shields from the hail of assorted missiles. The stairway up to the Threes was similarly barricaded, but the last flight up to the top landing far less. By the time we started up there, the cons had been virtually routed—panic setting in.'

Walsh let a pause elapse, ostensibly to make notes, before resuming. 'Officer Binton, why was it when you at last gained access to that top landing that you charged off on your own to the recess at the extreme north end of the landing?'

'I didn't, sir.'

'Oh?' Walsh glanced again at his DI, then flipped back through his notebook as though to check a verbal 'Did you see one of your colleagues do that?'

Binton hesitated, breathed, raised up and back, his expression one of studied concentration before finally shaking his head in denial. 'Not that I can recall, no, sir. Mind you, when we finally burst through—stuff being flung at us from all sides, lot of noise and activity—well, it's not a time for noticing things like that.'

'Like what?'

'Like one of our number dashing off to check the furthest recess.'

Taff Roberts, watching the officer intently, had become convinced of two things: that his curt self-assurance was in fact a counterfeit, indeed that he was lying in his teeth, though whether through personal guilt or to shield someone else was unclear. Secondly, that the chances of tripping him into an indiscretion, much less bluffing him into any form of admission, were negligible. As Binton had himself hinted, he *knew* about interrogation, and not only the procedures but also the ploys and pitfalls. Hence, aware of what Walsh was up to, the man was being careful to fine-tune his answers.

'I'm not saying no one did check it. That would certainly have made sense from the tactical angle.'

'How do you mean?'

'See, there was a great mob of cons all massed further along the landing.'

'South of the stairs?'

'Right, sir.' He nodded. 'So that was where the final action was going to be. But tactically sound for one of us to check there wasn't a load of cons hiding along in the recess ready to pile out and attack us from behind.' He paused, nodding at the probability of it. 'It's on the cards one of the lads would have thought to do that, sir, but it wasn't me.'

'The PM's getting restive, Roy.'

The Secretary of State had suggested they meet on the riverside terrace alongside the House, remarking that such an unseasonally fine morning should not be wasted. The tide was in flood, the water lapping grey-brown lips against the embankment stones close below their feet.

'We can't expect the Opposition to hold off indefinitely.'

'Agreed, sir. But don't forget they've burnt their fingers often enough in the past over prison matters. They know it's a two-edged sword.'

'Ah. Which, like that of Damocles, hangs over us all.'

'How true!' Roy Grantley's fluting chuckle merged with the shrill clamour of a flock of gulls in noisy contention around a passing garbage barge.

'None the less, the PM wants a further statement, if only to head off the lunatic fringe.'

'Understood, of course.' To the Whitehall mandarin, this whole delicate process, so regularly played out, was akin to an elaborate chess game. 'I spoke to Governor Hanford this morning. I'll have his report by lunch and a digest will be in your hands—er, the report, not the lunch—will be with you in good time for a statement at question time.'

'Good.' Peter Savage cocked his head. 'What about the CID investigation?'

'Ah, well, some difficulty there, Home Secretary.' The bureaucrat had selected his phrase with care, it being parliamentary coding for *looming danger*. 'Of course, Hanford is hyper-sensitive. Prison governors, no matter how blameless, hate to have coppers poking about within their walls.'

'*But*, Roy?'

'We had been given to understand the case against the prisoner was as good as made. However, Hanford now says the CID are demanding to interview some of his Mufti officers.'

'On suspicion, you mean?' Then, answering himself: 'Have to be, I suppose, coming so late on.'

He paused as a Thames tug gave throat with a double toot in warning to an approaching pleasure craft. The fragrance of lunch from the restaurant kitchens below, as though spiced by the bright morning, rose enticingly to his nostrils. 'Last thing anyone wants is that sort of trouble.'

Roy Grantley murmured agreement, aware that *anyone* meant specifically the PM. Yet the various interested lobbies were equally sensitive on the issue. Indeed, paradoxically, Grantley himself was almost alone in secretly welcoming the extended investigation, if only for the flap it would provoke. For it was in the containment of such developments that he and his fellow mandarins enjoyed an exhilarating power boost.

'The senior investigating officer is a man called Walsh.'

'Chief Super?'

'Yes. Dependable, so I'm advised, if inclined to be a shade pernickety.'

'Eh?'

'Let's say, over-zealous. Not, however, to the extent of being unrealistic.'

Peter Savage grunted, decoding this to mean, if not fully malleable, certainly open to the exigencies of expediency. 'Let's hope you're right.'

'I'm taking certain precautions, Home Secretary, to ensure the matter.'

CHAPTER 11

'Ronnie, old darling, you look simply dreadful.'

'Had a bad night.'

'Oh yeah? Come on, wanker, own up!'

Hythe shook his head but before he could repeat the denial, one of the officers was waving for him to get a move on. He broke into a rapid jog, gesturing for Tony to follow him and completing a couple of full circuits before slowing for his mate to pull alongside again.

'The screws are putting round the word that you're copping a manslaughter plea. That's not right, is it?'

'I told you already, Tony.'

'I know you did. But I thought maybe they'd put the heat on you to carry it.'

'Eh?'

'The screws, you pratt. Putting the heat on you because they're scared and want it all stitched up quick.'

'Yeah, well, I sure got that message.'

'Been round you, have they? That why you're looking so rough?'

'You know that new landing officer.'

'Big butchie with the crew cut?'

'That's right. He's the one.'

'Hythe!' The shout cut across, sharp and relentless, to slice like a blade between them. 'Time's up!'

'Grendon, Ron!'

'Eh?'

'Think strong like they taught you in Grendon.'

It was after one o'clock, towards the end of a plodding interview with Principal Officer Harker, before the expected phone call came through. Taff Roberts answered it, then scribbled a note that the DACC wanted a word at the chief's earliest convenience.

'It's not clear, Mr Harker, since you were leading Black section, how you came to be delayed getting up to the Fours.'

'I was commanding the section, sir: coordinating the action, giving the orders, not belting out front like a dumb hero.' He sniffed, rubbing at his nose as he shook his head in rejection. He was a tall, lanky man with iron-grey hair and an austere manner. 'Not my place to risk getting meself laid out. Leave the action to the youngsters.'

He paused to meet Walsh's gaze with a stare as stolid as his tone. 'By the time I did get up the top, all my lads was flanked shoulder to shoulder against the mob down along the centre of the landing. Certainly wasn't none of 'em along at the far recess.'

Walsh stood up to see the man out, wearied by the bland predictability of it—all too rehearsed and copybook for credibility.

Taff had the phone poised in readiness as he returned from the door. 'Okay, guv'nor? Assistant Commissioner?'

Walsh pulled a face but nodded. 'When rank calls.'

He poured himself fresh coffee, reaching his desk in time for Taff to hand him the receiver.

'Walsh here, sir.'

'Yes, Jack. What progress?'

Blaize's tone was deceptively affable; concealing his irritation, Walsh thought, over Hanford's latest complaint.

'You received the copy of Ronald Hythe's statement, sir?'

'I have it here, yes. Dead shaky, I'd say. Just the sort of fiction one'd expect from a villain in his situation.' There was a pause. Walsh caught the sound of drumming fingers. 'I take it you've got no corroborative evidence.'

'Not as yet, sir, no.'

'Well, that's it then, Jack. Charge him and have done.'

'With respect, sir, I'll do it my way, thank you.'

'Which is?'

'Currently we're questioning the officers engaged in the Mufti action up on the top landing.'

'Ah.' Pause. 'On the principle that, if you omit to do so, Hythe's defence counsel will demand to know why, hm?'

'Something like that, sir.'

'Something? I don't understand. You're surely not giving any credence to this story of Hythe's? A man serving life for a brutal murder, a man with a history of psychiatric disturbance, no shred of corroboration re this *alleged* officer.'

Another pause, the finger-drumming now the more audible—as was the suppressed frustration when he resumed. 'Jack, there's pressure on me from the Secretary of State's office. Couple of hours time, he's due to make a statement about the riot. Be useful if he could add that Hythe's being charged.'

'Premature, sir.'

'The DPP says he can shoot someone along to Brentford to review the evidence.'

'Not yet, sir, no. Sorry.'

Another final pause before: 'Jack, I'll see you at the Savoy this evening, just try and bring me some good news.'

Walsh's groan was plaintive as he rang off. Taff waited to catch his eye, then grimaced in apology. 'Sorry, guv.'

'Why? Men like Frank Blaize, they're just—' He cut off the criticism and instead stood up. 'Lunch—come on.'

'Right, guv. Why don't we nip along for a Bag o' Nails special.'

The DI was by no means sure that Kate Lewis would be there. They had left it all rather iffy that morning: if she could slip away from the Angels case; if Taff could slip away from the prison; if he judged that Walsh was in a sufficiently receptive mood . . . Not that he could ever hope to be sure of the latter; for all the cases they'd shared, his chief's moods remained largely an enigma. However, since Walsh had got it spot on about Kate getting Taff all bright-eyed and bushy-tailed, to heck with caution.

'Hey, look who's here!'

'Surprise, surprise.'

'Honest, guvnor, she's okay. Honest.'

'Oh yes? Known many reporters, have you?'

With which, tossing his coat to Taff to hang up, he strode across to where Kate was seated at the further end of the bar.

'My DI seems to think you're trustworthy, Miss Lewis. Right about that, is he?'

Kate shrugged, meeting his eyes, yielding only a partial smile with her answer. 'Where Taff's concerned, yes. He's worth compromising my professional ethics for. But as for you, Chief Superintendent, best not count on it.'

Walsh conceded a grin, then nodded towards the bar. 'In that case I'll have a double Scotch and keep my mouth shut.'

Before modernization, the pub must have been grotty and cramped. Now, with one central bar serving an open-plan saloon and with mahogany, brass and cut-glass styling, it had the illusion of a comfortable Victorian tap-room.

Taff joined them with a wry grin for his chief and a kiss for his girl. 'You two agreed to be friends?'

'A truce.'

'I'm allowed to buy the drinks.'

She did so and then, dismissing Taff's protests, ordered them the scampi special as well.

'Let her. She'll get it back on expenses.'

'He's right, Taff.'

'Of course I'm right . . . Money to burn, you media people. Money to bribe with and all. Cheque-book journalism. All those notorious villains down the nick, coining it in from the Sundays.'

'Sorry, Chief Superintendent, but you're out of date on that. The Press Council have at last managed to stop all that now.'

There was a pause, Taff wondering by what quirky urge he kept arranging these confrontations: the instinct of the subordinate to confess and be absolved? The urge of the young buck to flaunt his conquest before the old stag?

'So what have you got for us, apart from Scotch and scampi?'

'Give it a rest, guv'nor.'

'Not that it's any good you looking for a *quid pro quo*, Miss Lewis.'

'I wouldn't dream of it.'

'Quite right.' Walsh grinned, warming to her despite his antagonism. 'So?'

'I've got really very little—other than the impression of a well-orchestrated cover-up.'

'Oh?' If he agreed with her, the copper gave no hint of it. 'How?'

Kate hesitated, wary of revealing what little Taff had told her. 'For one thing, the Home Office are playing it all far closer to the chest than usual. Tighter than those oysters over there. For another . . .'

'Yes?'

'Well, my beloved editor seems unusually keen to get me away from Brentford and on to other stories.'

'The Hell's Angels?'

'Look, even if the trial had gone ahead, it wasn't going

to give us much on the first day. Jury objections, legal submissions—unlikely the prosecution would even start its case.'

Walsh sipped his Scotch, his expression masked, leaving Taff to ask the question.

'Your editor—is he usually the type to yield to pressure?'

'Ideally, pressure should have the opposite effect. Publish and be damned, hurrah! But his powers of decision are limited. People above him with powers of veto: our lawyers, the controller, the IBA. Lawrence Cawley's a good editor, but he's also a pragmatist. Presumably he wouldn't have got the job otherwise.'

'And what about you, Miss Lewis?' Walsh asked evenly. 'Are you one for taking on the Establishment?'

'Not in a crusading sense, no. My sole criteria is whether I think the public should get the story—hear the full facts.'

'And that applies in this case?'

'Ah.' She met his gaze, sensing the challenge. 'I don't know sufficient details yet to be able to judge. For instance, all I know about your side is that yesterday you expected to charge a man and then you didn't. Investigations proceed.'

'You building that into your cover-up theory?'

'I did mention it to my editor.' She grinned, raising her glass to him. 'Was I right? Are you getting pressured from on high?'

The chief snorted at her brashness, then turned as the scampi portions arrived at their table. He drained his Scotch and accepted the offer of wine. Only when it was served and they were starting into the food did he resume, his gaze switching teasingly from Kate to Taff and back again. 'I'll say this, you two are a right couple of chancers.'

'She'd do us proud in the Force, eh, guv.'

'Yours, I dare say, lad, not mine.'

'Is yours so different, Mr Walsh?'

'About as different as our ages.'

'Weren't you a chancer as a DI?'

Walsh grinned at her, munching into the scampi, surprised to find he was enjoying himself.

'I'll tell you one thing though, girl: you're wrong to label it as a cover-up. That's sensationalizing it. What's happening at Brentford nick, it's just routine—just the system.'

System or not, Sod's Law persisted for Walsh and his DI that afternoon. Word had clearly spread to the other Mufti men. Although the CID officers had now received a full list from the governor of all eighteen, it was claimed that only half-a-dozen were currently on shift and of these three were on court escort duties. The remaining three, when they finally presented themselves at the incident room, offered identical replies, answering defensively, largely in mono-syllables, volunteering nothing. The only positive conclusion at the end of a negative and frustrating day was that all those Mufti officers they had managed to see had something to hide.

But, as Walsh summed it up when his DI dropped him off at his home that evening: 'If you and I worked in that dump, Taff, doing the job they have to do, buckling down on all those bloody villains day in and day out, damn sure we'd have something to hide.'

'*Quis custodiet ipsos custodes?*'

'Put with your usual erudition, you bastard.'

'Ta, guv. Enjoy your bash at the Savoy.'

'With Alison and Frankie? You're kidding.'

Kate's afternoon turned out no less frustrating, not least when she arrived back at the ITN newsroom to find Steve Smith in possession of the crime desk.

'Hell's Angels adjourned for another week, then.'

'Yes.'

'I thought Lawrence was packing you off up to Brum.'

'No.' Irritating that, since Steve obviously knew she'd

been off to Brentford, they should have to go through this pretence. Pray God that at least Lawrence had honoured the secret about her contact with Walsh and Taff. 'Did you speak to your POA chum again?'

'I rang him this morning and asked what happened about that prisoner and the manslaughter deal.' The deputy editor grimaced, gesturing in negation. 'Tanner got very cagey, said it had only been rumour on the prison grapevine. It was obvious he was hiding something.'

The researcher paused, tugging at his moustache as he eyed Kate in query. 'Anything your end?'

'Only the sort of blanket furtiveness typical of a cover-up.'

The man continued to eye her, his expression almost melancholy. He knows, she thought; he bloody knows! Lawrence has damn well told him!

Walsh gazed around the crowded Savoy reception room and sighed in dismal resignation. Mess Nights like this had never been his scene: the Yard memsahibs vying with each other for appearances and status; the creepers like Frank Blaize in their pompous element, while the doers like Walsh, conscious of their ill-fitting DJs, invariably drank too much.

To that end, Walsh intercepted a passing tray to replenish his Scotch and consoled himself that functions like this were best seen as PR ops for policemen's wives: women who generally got a pretty raw deal, living often as little more than grass widows with men who, on those occasions when they did manage to get home for the evening, would most likely start to work off their anxieties on their neglected ladies. It was, he had to admit, a pattern true of Dell, not least as the years had brought seniority.

In theory, things should have improved with the years. Rank should have meant fewer exams, fewer night-shifts and stake-outs, less leg-work; instead, these had merely been replaced by more paperwork and meetings and courses and supervision stints. Not that Dell had grumbled. Healthy-minded woman that she was, she had instead filled the vacuum by taking on private tutoring, evening classes and so on. The main loss, fundamentally, was that she and Jack simply knew and enjoyed each other less often than they would have liked. What could have been a full relationship was little more than the functional co-existence of two acquaintances.

'I just saw the Blaizes,' she murmured, joining him now so as to exchange her empty glass for his full one.

She looked a treat, he thought, the styling of her ash-blonde hair complementing her height and the fine bone structure of her face, while the revamped dress concealed the matronliness of her bum and contrasted subtly with her skin tone. Wearing exceedingly well, he decided, for all the neglect.

'Alison was distinctly frosty. Somehow, I don't think we're meant to join them for food.'

'It'll taste the better for that.'

'What's up, Jack? She was all of a gush yesterday.'

'Sure—well, circumstances change. Like, a moment ago I had a full glass.' He growled, looking around for the nearest tray, only to stiffen politely in face of the craggy patronism of Deputy Commissioner Dick Pollard.

''Evening, Mrs Walsh. Not drinking, Jack?'

'He's on the waggon, Mr Pollard. Like always in the middle of a big case.'

'Ah yes, Brentford nick.' The commissioner nodded, easing his cummerbund. 'As it happens, Jack, your name came up in conversation earlier. Had an inquiry from Klein Holdings, the finance outfit. They want someone for a senior security post. Right up your street if you're interested.'

He turned benignly to Dell, touching her shoulder. 'Your decision as much as Jack's, of course, depending on whether you see his retirement as country pub or City executive.'

'Rags or riches, eh, Mr Pollard?'

'Ha—too true.' He turned, the hand shifting to the husband's shoulder. 'Think it over. Come and have a chat when you've tied up this prison job.'

'Right, guv'nor. Will do. Thank you.'

'Don't leave it too long. Klein's will be wanting to know.'

And just how conditional, Walsh wondered as the big man eased away to grace the next group, how conditional was the one upon the other? Perhaps not at all; or perhaps totally. Perhaps Pollard would recommend him regardless; or perhaps the implication was for Walsh to wrap up the one or forget the other.

Dell was nudging him, her eyes bright. They had of course discussed his retirement prospects, had tentatively agreed to do some touring in a mobile home and then in due course start to suss out the job market. But their expectations had been relatively humble: nowhere near as grand as senior man to a City outfit like Klein's. That was style; that was choice.

'Well, Jack?' Blaize's plummy tones cut into his reverie. 'Brought me that good news, have you?'

'Been working at it, sir.'

'This Brentford case?' Dell asked, moving forward. 'We'd all like some news on that one.'

'Tomorrow, Mrs Walsh. Right, Jack?'

'Right, sir.'

'Charges against the little man Hythe, eh?'

'That's how it looks, yes.'

'Good. About time, too.' Blaize swung his dimpled smile on to Dell. 'Your old man's been misbehaving on this one. His last murder and he decided to change the rules.'

'Jack? How?'

'Apparently it's the press.' His glance flicked at Walsh. 'Been in informal contact with a television reporter.'

'Where did you hear that, sir?'

'Isn't it true?'

'Only in that I've received information from a reporter. I've certainly not given anything in return.'

'What information?' Then, reverting to Dell: 'Sorry, Dell, hadn't intended to talk shop on your evening out.'

Dell Walsh eyed him, then sipped her drink. She could sense that, for all his show of indifference, her husband was disconcerted.

'As it happens, it amounted to no more than viewing a couple of taped interviews which turned out to relate to the riot rather than our investigation.'

There was a pause, Walsh reaching for a drink, secretly relieved when Dell hugged his arm and smiled at the DACC.

'Typical of Jack, Mr Blaize. Always double checks everything—no stone unturned.'

'By heck, Katie gal, where've you been all my life?'

She laughed, wriggling closer, relishing the exquisite sense of relaxation and security which their bodily contact brought to her. Yet it was dynamic rather than passive, as though there was a shared exchange of energy and excitement besides the sense of calmness and confidence.

'A mutual sentiment, sir, she said.' And, in saying it she knew that, as much as physical, it was also—even more so —a mutual compatibility of needs and of personalities; the reassurance of knowing that, as well as relishing her body, Taff Roberts also considered and enjoyed and respected her as a person—the Kathy person, moreover, whom she was now increasingly rediscovering. Fantastic. Rediscovering, too, the dimension of fulfilment of which, in recent relationships, she had begun to despair.

'So what were your impressions of Papa Walsh?'

'Why?' It was off-putting to find his mind on the man. 'Does it matter?'

'Not unless you want it to.' Yet his tone said that it did matter. Perhaps his use of the word Papa indicated why: the kinship of the two men who, through the circumstances of their work, were so intimately attuned. Kate felt an ironic twinge of jealousy that at this moment of post-coital limbo, Walsh had intruded.

'I'm very ambivalent about him,' she conceded carefully, aware that it could be a case of love me, love my chief. 'He's obviously very shrewd, very perceptive; but at the same time a man of strongly held views, dogmatic, even prejudiced.'

'Ah-ha, towards the press, aye.'

'And women, I suspect.'

Taff snorted. 'He certainly reckons he's hag-ridden at home. Wife and two daughters, although the eldest one's married.'

'You like him, don't you.'

'Mostly, I do. When he's on the job—sleuthing, question-ing, assessing, sussing out possibilities, rooting out the facts —great. Just so long as he keeps his complexes out the way.'

'Complexes?' It seemed almost ludicrous, given the latent strength and domination of the man she had encountered at lunch. 'How?'

'Oh, I don't know. Maybe it's just this case that's got me thinking that way—or else the fact that he's nearing retirement.'

'Or maybe it's you, Taff Roberts.' Then, at his bemused snort: 'You outgrowing your mentor.'

'Ha, that'll be the day.' He sniffed, fidgeting in discomfort, uneasy at the suggestion. 'Tell you what, Mistress Kath,' he resumed, moving close again, 'I'll answer you that just the moment we've wrapped up the case.'

'Did you mean that about tomorrow, Jack?' Dell felt the increase in the speed of the car and knew it reflected irri-tation; yet she persisted at him regardless. 'What you said to Frank Blaize about charging that prisoner . . .'

'Wouldn't have said it else, would I.'

'I thought perhaps you just wanted to get Blaize off your back—didn't like him mixing business with pleasure.'

Walsh grunted, considering the evening to have been

closer to an ordeal than a pleasure, as reflected, indeed, by
the fact that it was he rather than Dell who was now driving
home, as sober and keyed up as he had been when they'd
arrived at the Savoy.

'With Frank Blaize, everything's business—his blessed
career.'

'It all sounded a bit touchy to me.'

'You're right, love, it is.'

'But you meant what you said?' Pause. 'You'll get it
finished with tomorrow?'

She felt the car's speed increase even more. Next thing,
she thought, the silly twit'll get himself breathalyzed and
land himself in real trouble.

'What about that Klein Holdings job?' he asked suddenly.
'Fancy getting into the big money, do you?'

'If that's what you want, Jack.'

'You've certainly earned it, putting up with me all these
years.'

'Without you, you mean!'

'Yeah, that's right.' He paused, slowing down, shaking
his head in silent decision before: 'The answer's yes.' Then,
at her questioning glance: 'I'll be charging that little pratt
of a lifer tomorrow. Murder.'

Ronald Hythe hovered in the limbo state between waking
and sleeping. He would have lain fully awake but for the
numbing fatigue of the previous night's insomnia; he would
have been deeply asleep but for the dread terror which,
despite all his attempts at Grendon Think, still clutched like
a tight fist inside him.

He was tormented with half-dreams that his name was
being called out over the cell-block tannoy system . . .
half-dreams which, when he awoke in alarm, had him
convinced that Sheila and Phyllis had returned to plague
and haunt him.

Fantasies swam in and out of his consciousness: Tony

Rogers smirking and teasing . . . the landing officer squatting obscenely in the cell doorway . . . and then the joints, smoking the reefer joints . . .

The first one from the officer, yesterday's one, he had tried to dispose of by pushing it out of the grid over his cell window—a mistake since it had simply dropped down outside to lie on the ledge, visible for anyone looking out to see. Hence, with the second joint—the one he had found on his bed when he had returned with his toilet bucket after evening slop-out—he had been more thorough. Standing on his chair, he had shredded it into pieces as he pushed it out through the grid. And it was while doing so that he had noticed the traces of white powder rolled inside it . . . powder which, when he dabbed a minute amount on to his tongue, tasted sinister sweet.

The fantasy of now smoking the joints almost lulled him beyond the limbo state: he was tingling, he was beginning to slip away, slipping backwards, as though on the operating table, the anæsthetist pouring ether on to the mask over his mouth and nose . . . the stench of the fumes pungent and nauseating and . . .

Suddenly he was awake, his mind wrenching to consciousness, his body tensing, heaving him up on to one elbow to sniff in a frenzied escalation of fear as the dread nature of the smell reached him: not ether—not ether but petrol—the stench sweet and heavy in the close air of the cell.

For a moment of abject panic he was incapable of movement, his limbs locked rigid. Then he caught the stealthy movement at the door. The sound triggered action. He lurched from the bed, flung himself across the cell. He gasped breath down his throat, managed a strangled cry, his fists starting to flail impotently against the heavy steel door—and in that same instant, with a whooshing roar of combustion, the cell erupted into a huge ball of fire, flame which engulfed and enfolded him, searing the hair from his skull, blinding the sight from his eyes, congealing the screams in his throat, burning in a crescendo of livid pain across the skin of his legs, his arms and then his face as he flung himself instinctively down to roll across the blazing floor rug towards the bed.

DAY FIVE

CHAPTER 12

The cell fire, while exceptionally fierce, was contained before it could cause any structural damage, in the event destroying only the interior of Ronald Hythe's cell.

One reason for this, although there was no mention of it in the subsequent fire report, was the prisoner's single desperate scream just before the eruption of flame. That scream roused the inmate in the adjacent cell sufficiently to register first the ensuing gasps from next door and then, as he strained to listen, to sniff the distinctive smell of smoke as it seeped into his own cell through the gaps left when the central heating pipes had been installed.

His own frantic bellows promptly roused the man next along who also took up the cry, and so on, until the landing officer at last responded.

Even then, because of the security rule which excludes night-shift officers inside the cell blocks from having keys, there was a further delay while the landing officer radioed outside for the control room to contact the orderly officer. It was a further couple of minutes before he could get across from the orderly room and, leaving a dog-handler at the entrance door of the wing, dash up to the Threes to join the four night-shift men and at long last get Hythe's cell door unlocked.

By then, what with the fire bell, the shouts and spreading smoke and fumes, a thrill of panic was racing through the huge cell block at the ultimate terror of being trapped in an inferno.

Not that any of the inmates were unfamiliar with cell fires; it was seldom that a couple of months passed without one. The difference about this latest blaze, however, apart from its intensity, was the timing: for almost invariably a prisoner would choose to ignite his mattress and possessions during the evening shift when the officers were in possession of keys.

Although it was still several hours before slop-out time, there was precious little sleep for anyone during what remained of the night. Despite the continuing hubbub of men calling out cell to cell, few missed the sound of approaching sirens, first of the fire brigade and then, soon after, the ambulance. Those with cells on the west side of the wing were able to peer down as the stretcher was rushed out by nursing officers.

Word of the victim's identity spread rapidly throughout the wing. The shock of it hit Tony Rogers with a sharp pang. He lay sobbing bitterly in the darkness, his mood twisting from anguish to guilt and finally to a frenzied rage. They would pay for this! By Christ they would!

Tony had long since ceased to be a man of action, his resolve eroded by the drab, unvaried years of a life sentence commenced while he was still in his early twenties. Indeed, that residue of passion and self-esteem which still survived in him he owed largely to Ronnie Hythe, their closeness and trust. More, he owed him love—a love which his own oppressive sense of betrayal over Jason now warped to a spontaneous vow of vengeance.

But how? What hope of revenge in a regime where power lay with the officers, one of whom, through his abuse of that power, must now be exposed? Moreover, it was a regime which would be as implacable and vengeful against Tony Rogers as it had just proved to be against his mate Ronnie. Tread lightly, he told himself as the ambulance siren dwindled into the dawn; take care, Tony-O, or they'll barbecue you the same. They'll suss you as a threat and be watching you just as they were watching him.

As it happened, the circumstances at least of Tony's confinement were due for radical improvement that morning. Following a POA meeting with Home Office negotiators, the wing officers had now agreed to suspend their go-slow action. Thus, for the first time since the riot, A Wing's normal workday routine was being resumed, with the result that, after ablutions and breakfast that morning, Tony Rogers assembled with the rest of the work party destined for the print shop.

It was a grand title for a shabby set-up: a couple of obsolete presses, served by a lead font worthy of the ark; an arrangement so antiquated that even the more zealous print unions couldn't seriously oppose it as a threat to the livelihood of their non-criminal members. It was run by a civilian instructor, a retired master printer who extracted wonders from the two presses, machines for which he had a deal more respect than most of the offenders assigned to their operation.

As a civilian, the instructor liked to distance himself from the officers and their discipline regime—a fact which Tony considered could qualify him as a possible courier for a 'stiff', a letter smuggled out in evasion of the censors. But how to proposition him?

Eventually Tony decided to appeal to the man via a red-band trustie prisoner with whom the instructor was on chummy terms. Nothing doing. Instead the red-band came up with an alternative scheme—one far less appealing to Tony since the price, as he well knew, could be nauseatingly high. Yet no, for Ronnie—indeed, also for himself, to purge his sense of guilt and betrayal—no price was too high.

'Hi there, Wayne.'

'What you after, Angel Face?'

'Keep it down, you git.' Tony had waited until he could

corner the black beast in the relative privacy of the paper store. 'I want a favour, okay?'

'You're askin' *me*?' Wayne chuckled, shaking his head. 'Man, this got to be my lucky day.'

'Just shut the rap and listen, will you. The trustie says you're due up before the board of visitors today.'

'S'right.'

'Okay, I've got a stiff I want you to give 'em.'

Wayne blinked, his gormless mouth sagging open in incomprehension. 'Eh?'

'A stiff, you black git. A letter.'

'Man, I'm up there on application, not takin' tea with 'em.'

'You know the form: you'll be stood there at the end of the table with their worships all sat round. You'll have the letter up your shirt ready for the right moment. Then you step forward to the table, slide it across to the nearest geezer and tell 'em it's a special written statement. Easy.'

The mouth was open again but now in hilarity, laughter wheezing out in a blend of comedy and derision. Tony gripped his arm, shaking him, yielding himself to a nervous giggle as he tried to hush him down.

'It's been done before! Confidential stuff. Wayne, will you bloody listen!'

'I'm listenin', man,' he gasped. 'And what I'm hearin' is what them screws goin' to do to me afterwards.'

'You'll get paid, mate, don't worry. Paid plenty.'

The laughter promptly checked, the rubbery lips twisting in the travesty of a grin. 'For sure, man, for sure.' Then, with a sudden frown: 'Here, what's this stiff goin' to say?'

'Best you don't know that.'

'To do with the roast turkey, eh?'

'You what?'

'You wanting to tell 'em how the screws killed your little mate?'

Tony let go, swinging away, face averted. Whereas he knew Ron's death was a probability, he still clung to the coming of that ambulance and the fact that it had raced away with siren blaring.

He tensed, startled as the big West Indian gripped his shoulder, his voice oddly low.

'Okay, I'll take it. And listen, man, if it's for him, ain't no cost to pay.'

Jack Walsh was dour and silent when Taff collected him from home that morning. Liverish, the DI decided, overdid the drink at the Savoy beano last night—overdid it and ended up ranting about the case at poor Dell. And where to this morning? Back for another day of interrogating those Mufti bullies?

'Don't trust her, lad.' The remark came out of nothing shortly before the Chiswick roundabout.

'Guv'nor?'

'I know she's very dishy and all that, not to say a celebrity. No doubt she fancies you just as strong as you fancy her. Hurray. Beautiful. But she's a communicator and—'

'Guv, just do us a favour . . .'

'—and she's communicated about us.'

Taff waited until he had filtered them off the roundabout and into Kew Bridge road. It hurt—hurt like hell. 'Who to?'

'Presumably her editor.'

Another pause, Taff glancing sideways. To his surprise his chief's expression was nearer to regret than reproach.

'I got it from the assistant commissioner last night.'

'*Diawl!*'

'Well, there it is, lad.' Walsh sucked his teeth. 'Reporters.'

They checked in through the main gate of the prison, parked beside the Portakabin and walked along to the admin block and the incident room. Taff dialled the switchboard to check whether there were any messages, then blinked in surprise when Walsh told him to ring A Wing and get Hythe escorted over.

'What's the form, guv'nor?'

'Form?' The chief was abruptly curt. 'He's still our main suspect—still number one.'

That's a fact, Taff thought as he dialled the extension number for the cell block; and the Yard brass were all there last night at the Savoy to remind him about it.

The duty principal officer heard his request in silence and then connected him through to the deputy wing governor who gave him the news of the cell fire.

'Happened just short of five o'clock this morning.' The AG's tone was cold and dispassionate. 'The fire officer reckons he must have got hold of a bottle of something inflammable—paint thinners, most probably. They've got him in the burns unit at Mount Vernon Hospital.'

'How badly injured?'

'No news on that yet, but—well, from the state of his cell, I'd say he'll be lucky to pull through.'

The Mount Vernon Burns Unit sister ushered them straight through to see the houseman—a large, gawky man with prominent hands. His direct, cooperative manner came as a refreshing change after the sullen reticence of the previous few days.

'Rest assured, Ronald Hythe will live. No doubt of that. We've had them a lot worse from Brentford and Wormwood Scrubs in the past. It's premature to try and assess the extent of skin damage, but it's well under fifty per cent— well under. The main complication is that the primary burn areas were on the limbs and head, which is likely to mean an extended treatment period. A great many months. I'm afraid his sight is an unknown factor as yet; but in any event there's bound to be extensive facial disfigurement.'

'Is it possible, Doctor, for you to draw any conclusions from the nature of his burns?'

'Conclusions?'

'For instance, it's thought he got hold of some inflammable liquid.'

'Really?' The houseman sat back, the big hands joined mantis-like before him. 'We've had some self-immolations in here over the years, and I can tell you, wherever he poured the stuff, it wasn't over himself. He didn't *say* anything to us, although he was conscious before theatre. But if there was something like petrol involved, I'd expect that the main injuries were sustained from the initial combustion flash and that thereafter he must have lain flat on the floor.'

'That being so,' Taff put in, 'it sounds as if there could be a doubt about it being a suicide attempt.'

'You can certainly rule out the human-candle version. Also I can't recall a previous cell fire—most of which are a cry for help or a protest or even out of plain boredom—at such an ungodly hour. The likelihood is, if they try it in the small hours like this, they genuinely want out and they generally succeed.'

'So can we take it,' Taff persisted, determined to get it as clear as possible, 'that there are inconsistencies?'

'Not necessarily. For instance, it's possible he set it up as terminal—soaked his petrol or whatever into the bedding and carpet—but then had a change of heart after the shock force of combustion.'

'Foremost then, Doctor,' Walsh resumed, moving to stand up, 'how soon might we talk to him?'

'He's currently under mild sedation, also in shock, also doped up with painkillers . . . hence unlikely to be all that lucid. However, if you stay around this morning, we might be able to let you talk to him for a short time sooner or later.'

He stood up, reaching for his white coat as they moved to leave. 'One question, if I may: How come this is a CID investigation? Usually with cell fires we get the prison people coming to us.'

'No doubt you will about this one as well. Just so happens we were already investigating Hythe on suspicion of murder.'

'Ah.' The doctor peered at Walsh over his spectacles. 'So might that be a possible motive for suicide?'

'It's possible.'

'But then again,' Taff added, following his chief out, 'far from certain.'

'What's up, Philip?'

'A development at Brentford, sir. I thought you'd prefer to hear it now rather than wait till you break for lunch.'

Grantley had come out to meet him in the top corridor outside conference room D, currently in use for a selection board. He edged Knowles further away from where the remaining two candidates sat pretending to read the *New Statesman:* no doubt a couple more posturing cretins like all the rest they'd interviewed that morning. Heaven help the Service if this was the best they could shortlist at a time of unemployment.

'It's about the prisoner Ronald Hythe, sir. He tried to kill himself in the early hours of this morning. According to William Hanford, he set light to his cell at four forty-five a.m. Fortunately for him, the night staff were alert and on the prowl—by no means guaranteed at that hour—and got him out alive. Rushed off to the Burns Unit at Mount Vernon, but there's some doubt whether he'll pull through.'

Grantley shuddered, horrified at the prospect. 'Poor devil. Ghastly end.'

'There'll be the usual inquiry, of course. Findings available to the coroner should he die. Hanford anticipates ample witnesses re Hythe's state of mind.'

There was a pause, the senior mandarin still frowning in distraction at the horror of it. The nightmares which sometimes afflicted his sleep often featured situations where he, too, was trapped.

'His what?'

'Hythe's state of mind, sir—witnesses that he was depressed and suicidal.'

'Ah. Poor devil, what a way to choose.'

'Not all that many options, sir, not inside.'

'No.' Grantley felt mildly sick, sweat prickling across his skin. Hang it, what a business . . . and somehow representative, moreover, of the whole sordid rigmarole of prison. The Service, although offering no shortage of challenges, often seemed one endless cycle of unremitting gloom, degradation and futility: a political albatross, concerned with society's rejects, staffed by men more likely to be brutalized than uplifted by their thankless work, fraught with a chronic shortage of funds, prey to cut-backs and compromises . . . oh dear, dear. It was at times such as this that Roy Grantley erred towards the unthinkable, longing to yield to the separatist lobby and let the whole Prison Department go —let the prison unions have their head, let the whole abomination cut adrift from the Home Office and good riddance.

'Well, it's an ill wind, Philip.' He started back along the corridor. 'If nothing else, it'll ease the pressure on the Home Secretary.'

'Sir?'

'If poor Hythe's dead, that should at least round off the CID investigation.'

'Let's hope so, sir.'

'Hope what? That he dies?'

'Gracious no, sir.'

Tony Rogers tried to hide his terror in the workshop toilet. He managed to stifle the spasmodic sobs of panic rising in his throat but, although gripping tight to the seat, he was still unable to keep from shaking. He knew now—knew for a certainty that he'd blown it. His one and only step out of line—his first and last gesture of defiance—and all for what?

A futile gesture of heroism that would bring nothing but persecution. Frame-ups, beatings, cell spins, fit-ups for the Block, adverse reports, forfeiture of remission . . . the whole arsenal of screw retaliation. And all for what? For a dead mate and a rotten bloody conscience!

The realization had sunk in, becoming starkly obvious within minutes of the officers' arrival to escort Wayne off to the Board of Visitors hearing: Wayne the creep, the arse-licking grass! Of course he'd agreed to take the stiff; of course he'd pretended about doing it free! Here, guv, something I got from that burke Rogers . . . And even if he didn't, even if he kept his word and actually stuck it in the hand of one of the Board—so what? No question about whose side *they* were on. Magistrates mostly. Establishment. Glance at the note, raise those well-groomed eye-brows, then zip it straight off to Bully-Bill Hanford. Dear Christ, talk about stupid! As a plan it stood about as much chance as a one-legged man in an arse-kicking competition.

'You can come and have a short talk with the patient now.'

'Thanks, Doctor.'

Walsh started to fold away his case notes but paused as the medic added: 'He was extremely negative until I told him you were here. Until then he wouldn't speak or show any sign of animation whatsoever.'

The burns ward, a prefab hut abutting on a long corridor which linked numerous other prefab huts, had a sterile area just inside the entrance where they were asked to get togged up in green robes, skullcaps and face masks. They also had to get past the first of the prison officers who was sat drinking coffee with a uniformed police guard.

'Excuse me, sir, I need written authorization.' He stood to bar their way. 'Sorry.'

'You know me, Officer. You also know DI Roberts. You escorted a man over to us from A Wing. Connolly, I think it was. Now just skip the red tape.'

'Regulations, sir—high risk, Cat-A prisoner . . .'

'Who is right now even less capable of taking to his toes than you are of using your brain.'

'We're not only here to stop him absconding, sir, but also for his protection from the public. Vengeance attacks and that.'

'Well we're not going to do him over, Officer, so you can just sit yourself down or I'll get this police officer to arrest you for obstructing a CID investigation.'

They left the prison officer, red-faced with indignation and dialling through to the prison, while the doctor led them along to a partitioned section at the furthest end of the ward. Seated outside it was the second officer, robed like themselves and reading a girlie magazine. Walsh told him to go and take a coffee break until they were finished; but once again it took their warrant cards and officious threats before the man would go off to join his mate.

As it was, when the two CID men at last eased their way in with the doctor between the partitions around the bed, the object of all this pedantic security appeared not so much human as some sort of grossly swollen Sci-Fi specimen. He was laid out naked on a warmed water-bed; the skin of the torso, where it had been covered by the vest and underpants he'd worn to sleep in, was blotchy red; the rest of him—the arms, hands, legs, feet and head—was all layered with putty-coloured, open-mesh gauze through which suppura-tive fluid glistened like sweat. The only conventional therapy was the fluid drip into the vein and the twin pads over the eyes.

To Taff, unfamiliar with such acute-burn treatment, it came as a shocking prospect. He hung back, busying himself with notepad and pen, trying not to gag at the stench of singed flesh and disinfectant permeating his face mask . . . impressed, too, by the calmness with which his chief moved to sit beside the bed and lean towards the grotesque mask of Hythe's face. He glanced up for a nod from the doctor before speaking gently into the inflamed right ear.

'Right, lad, it's the copper here—DCS Walsh. What's all this, then?'

There was a pause, the blistered lips opening with pained slowness. The voice, when it came, was at first faint and halting.

'Any screws to hear us?'

'None. Sent 'em all packing. Just you and me, the doc and my DI.'

'Sure?'

'Straight up, lad.' Walsh glanced sideways to check that Taff had his pad ready for notes. 'Okay, so why'd you do it?'

'I didn't, guv. Honest to God.'

Hythe paused as though gathering his strength. Then, the hoarse voice issuing in a cracked monotone, he began to relate the horror of his ordeal: the finding of the joint and then the white powder inside it; the awakening in the dark to the reek of petrol fumes; the desperate panic as he rushed to the door before the fearsome burst of flame from which he had sought refuge by rolling blindly across to lie flat under the bed.

'Why, Ronnie?' Walsh's gaze flicked to his DI before he resumed to the figure on the bed. 'Why would anyone want to do this to you?'

'Obvious! 'Cos of that statement. 'Cos I refused to carry the shit can for the Mick's death.'

There was a croaking intake of breath which Taff realized was an attempt at a laugh. 'Know what, guv? I'd decided to change that statement. Scrap the bugger and pretend I'd done him in anyway. Go for manslaughter like Mr Spink wanted. Too bad, eh. Left it a bit late.'

There was a pause. Looking up from the notes, Taff saw the sweat beading across his chief's brow beneath the green rim of the skullcap. Abruptly Walsh glanced up from the burned, sightless man on the bed as the doctor held up a single finger and mouthed the words '*One minute.*' The chief gave a curt nod, then again leaned close to Hythe.

'You swear it before God, lad? You had no intention nor made any attempt to take your own life?'

'Before God Almighty, guv.' Then, the weird voice rising in urgency: 'Listen, I've been down that road: before Grendon, those two bitches nagging on and on at me to end it all, the same way I put an end to my missus. But that's all in the past, see. Grendon showed me how to put all that behind me—Sheila, Phyllis, all that suicide crap, all of it.'

He paused, the grotesquely swollen, suppurating head shifting on the water-bed as though in denial before adding: 'Mind, that's not what they'll say in the report. Not at all.'

'Report?'

'Guv'nor'll report that I tried to top myself. Witnesses, evidence from the shrink; evidence from me and all if that's what they want.'

'From *you?*' The question slipped incredulously from the doctor. 'You—you mean pretend?'

'Anything for a quiet life, Doc.' Then, with a repeat of the awful, croaking laugh: 'Anything for life.'

'But . . .'

'Tell him the system inside, guv. Tell him how things work.' He paused, attempting to turn his head towards the houseman. 'Ain't no point squealing how it was a screw what roasted me. None. Same as there's no point telling 'em it was the same screw what done for bloody Doyle.'

The head rolled back towards Walsh, the cracked voice taking on a malicious irony. 'That's right, guv, innit? If I'd played the system 'stead of taking your advice, I wouldn't be laid out here like a blind-eyed jelly.'

The doctor leaned forward, indicating that time was up. Walsh nodded and then reached a hand impulsively forward, only to check just short of the scorched tissue. 'Listen, lad, if you *know* him—if you can ID this officer for us . . .'

'You think I'm so bloody thick as to tell you that? Now?'
The head waggled briefly in rejection with a repeat of the
ironic croak. 'This time, mate, I've got his message.'

CHAPTER 13

'Come and sit, Kate. Conference time.' The editor had it
all there in readiness: coffee, secretary, deputy editor. 'I
want to review the Brentford situation.'

'What I told you yesterday still applies.'

'Except that the Beeb scooped us rotten on that Birmingham drugs story—leaving both you and me with a lot of
egg on our faces and no progress to report on Brentford
except—'

'Lawrence, please . . .'

'—except what Steve's just come up with this morning.'

'Oh?' She had sensed the deputy editor's smugness: loung-
ing back as though it was his newsroom and the rest of them
there only on sufferance. 'So what's that?'

'Before Steve explains, I think it's only right to brief him
on what you told me yesterday.'

'Ah. Being as we're a team, huh? Mutual secrets and all
that?'

'Right.' Lawrence nodded and, ignoring Kate's blatant
sarcasm, proceeded to tell the deputy of her inside contact
with the two CID men on the case. Steve Smith grunted,
seemingly impressed, making a creditable pretence, Kate
thought, of hearing it for the first time.

'That's great,' he affirmed. 'So between us we're on to at
least two limbs of the monster: the fuzz and the screws.'

He paused, moving pointedly to a different chair as the
editor lit one of his little cheroots.

'Well, the latest from my POA contact is that the main
suspect, Ronald Hythe, tried to kill himself—set light to his

cell an hour or so before dawn this morning. Apparently he'd have died in the blaze but for the vigilance of a landing officer. He's now said to be comatose in hospital—life in the balance.'

He paused for Kate to take this in and then added Tanner's propaganda plug. 'My contact says cell-fire suicides are fairly standard, not least among homicidal nutcases like Hythe. He says it's a glaring example of a man who should have been in Broadmoor instead of Brentford. And, so long as this inhumane practice is allowed to continue, so too will tragedies and fatalities like this.'

'Not a fatality *yet*.'

'No, but Doyle is. And the wing staff are adamant that Hythe's latest action is a result of his depressive remorse over killing Doyle.'

'I understand you have some information relating to the CID investigation at Brentford prison.'

'That's right.'

'And you are, sir?'

'Kent. Jeremy Kent. JP on the Acton bench and a member of the Brentford Board of Visitors.'

He was more besides: like deputy headmaster of a comprehensive, husband to a Samaritan, father to three teenagers, taxpayer, voter; and a man who cared about individuals in a world increasingly beset with bureaucracy. But for the latter, he might not have given such priority to the note thrust at him by an illiterate, visibly scared black prisoner petitioning the Board that morning for reclassification. More, he would not have defied the Board's chairman over the fate of the note.

Fortunately for both Wayne and Tony Rogers, the passing of such a note had been sufficiently unusual for Jeremy Kent to get stubborn and resist the chairman's decision merely to pass it to the prison governor. Yet it had been a close call, touching as it did on such issues as the Board's function and answerability. As defined, the Board had a dual role: on the one hand as an extension of prison discipline, responsible for dealing with offences too serious for the governor's jurisdiction; on the other, acting as a watchdog to oversee the rights and conditions of the inmates. But to which of these did Tony's stiff apply?

To the chairman, a stipendiary magistrate and an authoritarian, the note was a blatant attempt to evade mail censorship and as such was in breach of prison regulations. To deliver it as requested would be to abuse the official trust placed in the Board, to undermine their relationship with the prison governor, already strained enough via their inquiries into the riot injuries, and to risk a precedent which might start a flood of similar illicit missives.

In reply, Jeremy Kent—a new boy on the Board and secretly a-quake at his temerity—had urged that as citizens they had a duty to communicate murder evidence directly to the CID officers on the case. It was for the police rather than the Board *or* the prison authorities to assess the validity or otherwise of the evidence. And therefore, with all due deference to the chairman, could not the fate of the letter please be put to a vote? Whereupon, having narrowly won, Kent felt he had no option but to volunteer personal delivery into DCS Walsh's hand.

The delivery task, since the CID men were no longer at the prison, led him in due course to Scotland Yard where bureaucracy promptly loomed. Formal courtesy at the reception desk, along with requests for personal identification, had finally yielded a young DI, reputedly from the same department as the chief super. It had been only with the utmost reluctance that the DI had agreed, in the absence of Mr Walsh, to contact the head of department with a view to Mr Kent's handing him the evidence in person. The lengthy wait outside DACC Blaize's office had led Jeremy Kent to question his zealousness as a citizen, murder case or not.

'I appreciate that as evidence it's no more than hearsay; moreover, hearsay from a convicted life-sentence prisoner who could well have motives for wishing to falsely incriminate the prison officer named in the letter. None the less, it's a lead of possible value to the investigating officer.'

'I'll pass it on, sir.' There was a blandness in the assistant commissioner's tone which Kent found less than reassuring. 'Much obliged for your assistance.'

'There's a rumour that Hythe was due to be charged with the murder of the Irishman.'

'Oh?'

'Three of us on the Board went into A Wing this morning to inspect the damage to Hythe's cell. The wing staff were most positive about it.'

'Prisons and rumours, sir.'

'Whether or not it's true, the fact remains that the officer named in that letter as having threatened Hythe was present on night-shift duty at the time of the cell fire.'

'You're certain of that?'

'Yes.' Kent pulled a face. 'Because, ironically enough, the wing staff are crediting him with having saved Hythe's life.'

'A hero, then?'

'Or else a thug whose attempt to murder Ronald Hythe mis—er—misfired.'

'Hello?' Ashley Pelham waited for the call-box pips to finish. 'Pelham here.'

'DI Roberts speaking, sir. Couple of points you may be able to help us with. First, is there any chance of you being able to get a look at the A Wing duty roster for last night? Landing staff.'

'Hm. Be easy enough if I could get into the wing office. But, being suspended, there's no chance of my even getting into the prison, much less the wing. What was the other thing?'

'About Ronald Hythe, sir: any possible way he could have

got hold of a pint or so of some inflammable liquid such as petrol or paint thinners?'

'Rather depends on whether the inmates are back on work duty and association yet.'

'They weren't up to yesterday, no. You see, Hythe was the victim of a cell fire around five o'clock this morning.'

'Oh dear God . . .'

'He managed to survive despite extensive burns. Your deputy told us he'd got hold of something inflammable.'

'Well, if so, with everyone banged up all the time—no work or association—the only possible source would have been from one of the wing staff.'

'Or alternatively, sir, *by* one of the wing staff.'

'Burned by one, you mean?' There was a pause as Pelham thought it over. 'Well, Lord knows it's a sickening prospect —revolting—but I have to agree it's a possibility. As you know, I didn't *like* Hythe. No one does much except young Rogers. But I wouldn't type him as suicidal—not since he had that year at Grendon. Of course, he *could* have got some petrol or whatever from an officer. But it's highly unlikely.'

He paused as the pips went, waiting until Taff had pushed in another coin before resuming.

'One thing, Inspector, even if I can get you the roster names, you're going to have a problem questioning the men. After all, a cell fire as such is none of your business. Initially, at any rate, it's going to be a prison matter, not CID.'

'It's arguable, Mr Pelham. But at least a sight of the names might give us a lead.'

'All right then, I'll try and find out for you.'

Kate Lewis was standing beside the pub's telephone kiosk as Taff rang off and pushed out to face her. There was an element of caution about her smile, he thought—caution or else guilt—or was it in fact his imagination, reading into her what he felt should be there.

'Glass of the usual?'

'Taff, I . . .'

'The chief's sitting over there. Go and join him while I get you one.'

He moved off to the bar, bought her a glass of Hock, then took it across to join them. Walsh's expression was noncommittal as he caught Taff's eye.

'Your press lady's well informed,' he remarked evenly. 'She knows about Hythe already—the cell fire.'

'Yeah? The old prison grapevine, eh.' He turned to her. 'Who's your source, Kate?' Then, when she hesitated, sensing his bitterness: 'Of course, that's something you'd be reluctant to reveal. Journalistic discretion and all that, eh.'

She met his gaze for a moment, then gestured in appeal. 'Okay, so what's with all the hostility?'

'Hostility?' Taff Roberts glanced at his chief, then back again at the woman who, over the past few days, he had so deeply wanted to trust. 'To do with discretion, perhaps. To do with betrayal of sources.'

Kate was suddenly flushed, her hand trembling as she went to sip her wine.

'Taff, love, I'm sorry . . .'

'Why? I don't recall you making any promises. I'm the bloody donkey here, not you.'

'I told you I was under a lot of pressure . . . and I—well, a reporter *has* to trust the editor. Has to. And then you see, this morning, with that snake of a deputy editor, he—'

'Except it wasn't this morning. It was yesterday.'

'Oh?'

'Yesterday evening, to be exact. The chief super got a roasting from his guv'nor.'

'Oh God.' She glanced at Walsh, then back in abrupt retaliation at Taff. 'Anyway, it wasn't a betrayal. All I did was tell Lawrence that we'd met—made contact—nothing more. Damn it, how could there be any so-called betrayal? You'd neither of you told me anything to betray!'

'Bloody good job we hadn't't!'

'Okay, Taff, that's enough.' Walsh had been watching as they tore at each other, silently weighing Kate's response. Now he reached out to touch her arm. 'Not a roasting, lass, just a mild rebuke.'

He turned to his DI. 'In all fairness, now, she has come across with a good bit of info for us.'

Then, resuming to the bemused Kate: 'You'll have to forgive that Welsh pride of his. It's that you've hurt, not his career.'

'*She's* to forgive *me*?'

'I'd be obliged,' Walsh persisted to Kate, 'if you could answer his original question as to where you heard of Hythe's getting burned.'

'From our deputy editor's contact with the officers' union. Psychotic depression; remorse over killing Doyle; saved from suicide by the vigilance of heroic landing staff.' She paused, reaching for her glass. 'Have you seen Hythe? Does that conform with what he's saying?'

Taff grunted, expecting his chief to tell her to stop fishing. But instead he shook his head, going on to tell her how Hythe had described the attempt on his life and also how a couple of the things the doctor had said tended to support Hythe's claim.

'Pelham as well, guv'nor, on the phone just now.'

'That so?' Walsh glanced bleakly at him before resuming to Kate. 'So there it is: if someone did try to kill Hythe—*if* so—then it has to be one of the officers on the landing staff.'

There was a silence. Staring at the senior detective, Kate sensed the change in him from the previous day: no longer merely a professional doing his job with maturity, astuteness and perception; today he was a man feeling his years and weighted with a burden.

'Why tell me that, Mr Walsh?'

'My question, too, guv'nor.'

'Because I want your deputy editor to leak it to his POA

contact. Tell him, Miss Lewis, that we've got hold of hard evidence incriminating one of the wing staff.'

They could hear the telephone ringing as they came back along the corridor outside the incident room. It continued to ring while Taff fumbled to get the door unlocked and dashed across to answer it.

'Ashley Pelham here about that night-shift query. I rang through to the A Wing office and spoke to Gavin Benson, one of the assistant governors. I'd always taken him to be on my side.' He paused, clearing his throat. 'Not any more. On the contrary, when I asked him who was on shift last night, he got very abrupt. Said he wouldn't tell me even if he knew and then promptly rang off.'

'Same as us,' Taff grunted, 'same as we've been hitting all week.'

'Anyway, I decided to have another try for you. I knew the chief's clerk would have received a USR form with what we call the out-turn detail listed on it. For records and the computation of overtime and so-forth. I thought there was just a chance he wouldn't know I'd been suspended.'

'Any luck?'

'No. He was every bit as cagey as Benson.' Pause. 'Sorry, but I'm afraid you'll just have to tackle Hanford direct.'

'Which,' Walsh muttered, reaching across for the other telephone, 'we already know is a non-starter.'

He dialled through to the Yard, asked for the DACC's extension and within a minute was briefing Blaize on the cell fire and the evidence in contradiction of its being an attempted suicide.

'We know all too well, sir, what the governor's response is going to be. So this time I'm applying in advance for the authority to override him. I want to question all four of the officers on last night's shift and I don't want Hanford blocking me.'

There was a lengthy pause. When it came, however, the

assistant commissioner's reply was reassuring in tone.

'Very well then, Jack. But I'm going to need chapter and verse on all this before I can tackle the Home Office. Best get yourself and Roberts over here. Bring everything you've got—verbals, tapes, the lot—and I'll see you here in an hour.'

As he rang off, Frank Blaize was already searching out a small contacts book from the top drawer of his desk. He buzzed through to his secretary for an outside line on the red phone. This done, he dialled through to the Home Office switchboard and asked for extension 284. It rang only once before Grantley answered.

'Hello, Roy—a quiet word with you on scramble, please.'

'Midday tomorrow, Kate, you're off to the Home Office for an interview with Roy Grantley.'

'Apropos of anything in particular?'

'You tell me.' The editor sounded distinctly defensive, Kate decided, as well he should do. 'When she rang, his secretary said you'd applied to see him earlier in the week.'

'The day after the riot, yes.'

'Well, presumably it's to do with that.'

The telephone interrupted them as usual: Snow from Beirut. It was several wildly expensive minutes later before the editor resumed to Kate, asking if she had anything new from her CID contact.

'One little item, Lawrence, yes. Something I happen to find distinctly sinister.' She sat down, eyeing him, waiting for the damned phone to interrupt again. 'When was it you first told Steve Smith about my contact with the CID?'

'You know very well—when you were in here this morning. Why?'

'So just who else did you tell before that? Like yesterday?'

'No one.' He gestured in dismissal. 'Well, the producer, obviously, but . . .'

'It was confidential, Lawrence.'

'My sweet, he would never . . .'

'He did—evidently. He did or you did. Somebody did. And now my man's in schtook for indiscretions to the media.'

'Oh.'

'*My* informant, Lawrence. *My* confidentiality blown. And for what?'

The editor sat back, shaking his head, but in dismissal rather than apology. 'A mystery.'

'Fantastic. So I'll raise it with the mandarin tomorrow and ask who it was who told him!'

'Hi, Taff. Still hitting Sod's Law?'

'Harder than ever, Harry.'

The department office was on the Yard's seventh floor, its open-plan layout resembling the newsroom of a national daily paper: rows of rubber-topped desks for the sergeants and DIs, ringed with glass-partitioned boxes for the senior ranks.

Taff grunted, dumping his load of files on Harry's desk and pulling a chair across for a heartfelt moan about the case.

'A right dog, mate.'

'Nicks are always trouble.'

'Sure. And right now there's something bloody odd going on upstairs with Gaffer Blaize.' Taff pulled a face, tapping the heap of files. 'We brought in all this stuff for a case session with him. But when we went in just now, he's sat there like Lord Justice Lane on a bad day. Said there'd been unforeseen developments and then sent me packing.'

'Sounds dodgy.'

'Like you just said, Sod's Law.'

Harry frowned, rubbing the back of his neck, hoping to heaven it had nothing to do with Kate Lewis. 'He didn't mention a bloke called Kent, did he?'

'No. Why?'

'In here earlier asking for your guv'nor.'

'What about?'

'He'd got some info of some kind. But he wouldn't trust it to the plebs—insisted on taking it upstairs.'

'Kent?'

'Jeremy Kent. Said he was a member of the Brentford Prison Board of Visitors.'

'I'm extremely sorry, Jack—not least since it's likely to be your last murder. No reflection on your ability, of course. Certainly won't prejudice your chances of getting that security post with Klein Holdings. None the less, it would have been nice to see you go out with a good Bailey conviction.'

Frank Blaize crossed from the cabinet to set a schooner of sherry on the desk. Walsh stared bleakly at it. In mediæval times, he thought, when they did this sort of hatchet job properly, it would have been a goblet of poisoned claret. Now they used Amontillado and Special Branch.

'Commander Johnson will be in to see you later on. Obviously he'll expect the fullest possible briefing.'

'Obviously.' Walsh tried the sherry. It tasted of rust. 'May I ask, sir, by what weird convolutions this case is now being classified as a matter of national security?'

'No need to talk like that, Chief Superintendent.'

'Like what?'

'Sullen—facetious . . . The plain fact of it—the reason for Special Branch now having to take it over—has to do with Doyle's IRA background.'

'Dog's meat, you told me.'

'Pardon?'

'Him and Connolly—dog's meat—a couple of second-rate bombers under the command of Evelyn whatsit.'

'So I was given to understand.'

'You told me you'd read the actual file, brought to you by special dispatch-rider.'

'I read *a* file. Read it in good faith. Presuming it to be *bona fide*.'

'Military intelligence deceived you? Is that what you're implying, Mr Blaize?'

'Implying nothing!' Then, less sharply: 'I'm merely suggesting that Doyle's IRA status may have been a lot more sensitive than—than it was expedient for either you or me to know about. And that this is the explanation why I've just received instructions to hand the investigation over to Special Branch.'

'If it was that sensitive, how come they waited five days before taking it over?'

'Clearly, Jack, because—in common with the Home Office and the Cabinet—they were hoping you'd do the obvious: namely, charge Hythe with manslaughter and have done. You didn't. Now you've had this development of the cell fire and you're wanting to investigate it as a possible attempt on Hythe's life and—'

'And the powers that be have decided enough is enough.'

'Whatever's been decided, Jack, it's not for you or me to question.' He moved impulsively to refill his own glass, hating Walsh, hating the situation and its implications, hating the whole palsied rigmarole. 'You'll hand over to Commander Johnson and that's an end of it.'

CHAPTER 14

'What did Taffie Roberts say?'

'Not a lot. I got the feeling he was half expecting it. Not a lot he could say, mind, what with that cloak-and-dagger commander sat there in my office waiting to be briefed.'

'And what did *he* say?'

'The commander?' Walsh crossed to pour himself another Scotch, avoiding Dell's eyes. 'He put up a reasonable show of interest. In fact, I could almost have believed he was going to pick the case up where we'd left off. Almost.'

'Well, why not?' Surprisingly, she held out her own glass for a refill. 'Why should he pretend?'

'Because, my love, there is no way he or any of his gumshoe oppos are going to carry this investigation a single step further. He and I were going through a dance of death together, and we both knew it.'

'But supposing—' she retrieved her glass from him and took a sip—'supposing what Frank Blaize said about Doyle and his security file was true?'

'It was a load of cods, Dell. That whole thing was just a face-saver.'

'How can you be so sure?'

'Because it's the system, that's why. Standard procedure. It ensures that in the unthinkable event of my going bananas, disobeying orders and pursuing inquiries regardless, then I can be dealt with—silenced, arrested, certified —in the interests of national security. It's the old, old stand-by.'

'I see.' She hesitated, reluctant to ask the next question but knowing it was central to everything—to his life and hers and to their future. 'And just how unthinkable is the unthinkable?'

For a long moment he didn't respond. He was staring at the photo triptych above the fireplace depicting his various career steps: as senior cadet at the passing-out parade; receiving his first bravery award as a DC; at the promotion ceremony to superintendent's rank. Abruptly he turned to sit beside her—not to touch her since he wasn't much of a one for touching—yet his expression alive with the intensity of his need to carry her with him and have her approval of what must now be done. It struck her as flattering, almost overwhelming, if at the same time as absurdly quixotic.

'Dell, I swear to you, if you could only have been there —seen that poor bugger lying there, skinned *raw* by whoever set that fire . . . seen him, heard him, *smelt* him . . . oh Jesus! . . . I mean, how the hell could I just fade away into sweet oppulent retirement, eh? No way, Dell. Not now.'

She hesitated to reply, sensing that his impassioned mood could easily swing against her—hoping, too, that young Heather wouldn't come crashing home before they could resolve it.

'You're sure?' she began carefully. 'You're quite certain this laddie Hythe wasn't, you know, conning you along?' Then, when he made no reply: 'They lie in prison, don't they? You told me that yourself. Lie as a reflex, you said. Lie almost like it was a religion. Well, Jack, maybe that's what this Hythe bloke's up to.'

'Yes.' He nodded, and she could sense his restraint. 'Yes, I sussed that possibility—Taff and me, we both of us did.' He gestured in appeal. 'Two hard-nosed coppers, used to dealing with villains and nutcases. The bad, the mad and the sad. Used to liars in every stripe, shape and flavour.' He shook his head. 'If Hythe was lying to us—well, then I'm Donald Duck.'

'So all right!' Dell took a bracer of Scotch, readying herself for the crunch issue. 'So you're saying he's innocent and last night's effort to kill him originated from the killer of Doyle—yes?'

'There's no other explanation.'

'And now you're off the case.' She waited for him to nod. 'And?' Then, when he left it to her to finish: 'And there's no way you feel you can retire with that on your conscience, hm?'

'No way.'

'Bloody hell, Jack, *why*?' It burst from her in abrupt exasperation. 'In thirty years in the Force you've seen worse than this—times over! You've told me about worse. You've *done* worse once in a while—when it's been the way things have to be done—which is no more nor less than what *this* is. So, I mean, for heaven's sake, what is all this about?'

She paused, glaring at him, only to persist over his reply. 'Don't let's kid ourselves now. You go on with this and you can just kiss Klein Holdings goodbye—same as you can any other security job, come to that. You blot it now, my lad, and you're blotted for good.'

Once again he went to reply and once again she persisted over him. 'Don't—please don't start telling me about justice. Justice to vindicate a ratty little murderer? Justice to nail some officer who's dedicated his life to warding society's villains? No, Jack Walsh, this is to do with *you*—to do with your bad conscience . . .'

'That's enough now, Dell! Just shut it now!'

'Your conscience,' she insisted, 'if not for the past, then because you feel responsible for that bloke getting burned half to death in his cell! *Right?*'

She paused at last, glaring at him in bitter defiance. And it was as well for them both—strong-willed and determined, yet as passionate about each other as about the separate views they now held—as well that, into their tense silence, there came a ring on the front doorbell.

DI Roberts was as yet only slightly drunk—sufficient to get him along to the Walsh household but not in reckless defiance. Not that he was there in the expectation of any sweeping resolutions. A dozen years of service—dedicated, diligent and rewarding—were not lightly to be shrugged away.

'So it's over then? Finished? Assigned to the spooks? Come on, guv'nor, we both know what that means.'

'Let's go down the pub, Taff. Dell's heard all this once this evening and damn sure she's not into hearing it all again.'

'Oh. Well, then . . .'

'Sit down, Taffie Roberts,' Dell cut in. 'I'm off round to Jilly's—off to tell her what a damn great fool her father is.' She picked up the bottle of Scotch, eyed the amount left in it, then thumped it back on the sideboard. 'If Heather comes in, send her round to Jill's.'

Walsh waited until he heard the door bang behind her, glad enough to have a cool-off period before finally settling it between them; glad, too, to have his DI round for a talk. While in no sense seeing himself as a crusader against the Establishment, he certainly didn't want a rash Welsh puppy under his feet while doing whatever it was obstinacy dictated had to be done.

'Findings to be left on the file—right, guv'nor? That's how it'll be. Open coroner's verdict on Doyle; suicide attempt on Hythe, like he told us himself; investigations proceeding *sine die* under Commander Spook. End of case for you and me.'

'That's about it, Taff.'

'So what did Dell mean just now about you being a fool?'

'Never you mind.'

'I want in, guv'nor.' Then, persisting with true *Land of my Fathers* rhetoric. 'We're a partnership—a team. Whatever you're at, it has to be together.'

'No, boyo, you've got too much to lose. Far more vulnerable than I am.'

'You reckon?' Taff sat angrily back and took a big drink. There was an element of relief there, yet at the same time a sense of deep hurt—the sense of rejection as though almost by a lover. The double such blow, indeed, within the one day: Kate's betrayal and now his chief's rejection.

'It's a rum old do, though, guv'nor. I mean, take that bugger Hythe: in the old days he'd have been topped for what he did to his wife. You've spent your life putting villains like him away. And look how often we've talked about how they should *still* be topping a good few of them!'

'So what?'

'Well, what I'm saying is, it's not exactly for him as a person, is it? He's only a—whatsit?—a cipher, right?'

'You're drunk, Roberts. Your tongue always gets the runs when you're drunk.'

'No, no, seriously, what you're doing now, it's—'

'Let's get this straight, lad, I don't bloody *know* what I'm doing—not yet. I've got no leads and fewer ideas.' He snorted, tugging at his eyebrows. 'Just a very angry wife.'

'Ah, right then, chief. Fine. You see, that's why I came round here—because I came up with a lead. Better than that, I got the devil's name.'

'You really are drunk.'

'No, listen to me, for heaven's sake! You see, Gaffer Blaize was given some evidence today from a man called Kent.'

'You what?'

'Never mind how I know, but he was and presumably he gave it to Commander Spook instead of to you. So then this evening I did some checking and managed to chase up this Kent geezer. You can call his number and hear it all direct. But what it boils down to is the name: landing officer, arsonist, Mufti man, the lot: Discipline Officer Binton.'

'Right then, brothers,' John Tanner said, 'just so we're one hundred per cent solid on that: the landing staff had been keeping a close eye on Hythe, what with his involvement in Doyle's death. They'd clocked his frame of mind, had twice reported suicide indications to the MO and got him on special observation. Then, early hours of this morning, Angus Binton's along for the half-hour check-up when he hears this sound of gasping from the cell. He hits the nearest fire button and then radios out to the control-room to alert the orderly officer. The OO gets across to the cell block sharp as he can, picking up a Zulu patrol on the way to hold the main key while he's inside. The moment he's up to the Twos and they get the cell door open, Binton crawls in with a fire hood and mask on and manages to drag Hythe out while the others are at it with the extinguishers.'

'What you at, then?' Ned Ballard was toying with his tankard, frowning over it. 'Putting Corporal bloody Binton up for an award, are you?'

'Don't be stupid, Ned.'

'Well then, why all this rehearsal?'

'Just so we all know what happened.'

'The official version, you mean.'

'Have you heard any different from that, Ned? Anyone else heard any different?'

'I heard those coppers were up at the hospital well before the wing deputy got up there. Heard that Hythe said a whole lot more to them than what he said to our lot.'

'That's right, John, that's what I heard, too.'

'Except, Reggie, that cell fire's no business whatsoever of the CID.'

'I just bloody hope not. 'Cos I'll tell you this: if butcher Binton's been up to no good and those two coppers are on to it, there's no way I or this branch wants owt to do with it.'

'Listen, Ned . . .'

'No, Brother Tanner, you listen to me. A good few of us on this executive don't like what's going on. Oh, acknowledged, you're a great one for seizing opportunities. Never miss a trick, that's you national executive people. Well, that's champion so far as it goes. But some of us reckon you're getting a mite too clever with all your wheeling and dealing.'

Tanner sat back to hide his discomfort behind a pull of ale. He'd had a nasty jolt earlier when that bloke Smith had telephoned from ITN to say the police had a strong lead. That had necessitated a panic call or two and some painful concessions as a result. All he needed now was old Ballard and Reggie Boothe starting a revolt by the wets.

'I'm not with you, Ned. We've had a massive riot—a lot of aggro to ride out. If you've got a beef about my handling of the situation . . .'

'No, John, none.'

'Well then?'

'Closing ranks for the lads is one thing. Solidarity's the name of the game, no question about that. But covering for a freakie sadist like young Binton, much less making him out a hero, brother—that's something else.'

*

Kate Lewis was depressed, her normal buoyancy and drive yielding to bleak introspection and doubt. Of what strength, after all, was her status? Kate who? Nothing more succeeds than success in the eternal insecurity of the media business and, likewise, the obverse lurks like an eternally menacing predator.

She had blown it badly over the Brentford story: got all defiant and scrappy with Lawrence Cawley; got, as he had put it, egg on both their faces over the Birmingham drugs story; pushed things to the limit with Steve Smith; dropped Walsh in it with his commissioner and Taff in it with Walsh, for heaven's sake!

Kate who? And worse—yes, for once worse even than that—Kathy who? For that's who she was to Taff, to her Welsh boy from the hills, to whom she had clung and with whom, almost uniquely of late, she had felt secure and whole and loved . . . but loved as Kathy, not Kate. And now that, too, was blown: he hadn't come, he hadn't telephoned; nor had he been home to answer her calls.

Her one hope was that his cold, bitter words at the pub had been made so harsh by the presence of his chief. Kate knew all about the chauvinistic obligations of policemen: the rugby-style loyalties on which Walsh must have played when telling Taff of her betrayal. She knew also that at heart, certainly when in bed with her, Taff had his other side which was sensitive and considerate and tolerant—anything but the Welsh-ram image which he doubtless only played up for his mates in the Force. She had built her hopes on this, praying that at least he would give her the benefit of a fair hearing rather than just slamming the door. But no: no call, no knock, no reply.

Around nine o'clock, running true to form, she had got through to Bill, her ex. He had listened in his role of father confessor, increasingly concerned as he sensed her pain and unhappiness. He had tried to commiserate, assuring her she wasn't alone or useless or hateful or shallow or selfish. It had helped Kate a fair bit . . . until, switching on *News at Ten*, she had realized she hadn't *done* anything since the riot and didn't look like doing anything more until the blessed Angels trial finally got started.

It was during the commercial break that the telephone rang. Kate stood staring at it, forcing herself to let it ring four times before picking it up. Wrong number: some twit wanting Mary, not Kate! And then, in the same instant that she banged down the receiver, another ring, this time from the doorbell. She checked her dress, checked her hair as she passed the mirror, paused long enough to slip the safety-chain on the door, then opened to peer out.

'Ah—a policeman but the wrong one.' She slipped the chain off and opened up, peering around in the hope that they'd come together. 'No Taff?'

'Sorry, no.' Walsh stepped inside, removing his coat, nodding as she took it from him and hung it by the door. 'Inspector Roberts is no longer on the case.'

'Oh?' She frowned in concern. 'Nothing to do with my so-called breach of confidence I hope.'

'No, Miss Lewis, nothing to do with that.'

'Good.' Pause. 'He's a pretty special fella, you know.'

'Everyone's got to be special to someone.'

'Don't pretend he isn't to you, too, chief.'

Walsh gave a rueful snort. Oh yes, he thought, all too special, like a blessed son. Getting at me with his renegade ideals, his naïve crusade for justice; pushing me to break the code, disregard the rules of a lifetime and stick my stupid old neck out like this, God help me!

He snorted again, pointing at her as he shook his head in mock rebuke. And yes, she thought, you could be pretty special yourself, foxy old devil.

'So why is he off the case?'

'Same reason I am.'

'*You?*'

He nodded, then asked for a Scotch and settled back to

outline the escalation of events since they had met earlier in the day. And what an irony, she thought, eyeing him as he talked, that he should now be here like this. Not five days ago the antipathy between them had been rigid with mutual distrust and contempt, assumptions of media deceit on his part and of corruption on hers. Yet now he was here *in extremis* to seek an alliance. And what more improbable and unholy alliance than top cop and media maid! Fantasy time. Certainly desperation time.

'So I was right,' she remarked when he had done, 'right about a cover-up.'

'As of today, yes.'

'Which means I'll be hard put to help: already muzzled over those two tapes you saw, and now they'll invoke the full national-security D-notice to legitimize it.'

Walsh grinned at her and shook his head. 'All I'm asking of you, girl, is to flush Officer Binton.'

'What?'

'Spook him—get him on the run. He's guilty and therefore he's vulnerable. All right, so he is also a very cool customer who's well aware of how the system works. For instance, he knows that, if only to protect their image, the POA will go a long way to shield him. More, that the Home Office and the present Cabinet will keep step with the POA—up to a point. Like, today, taking the investigation away from me and Taff. But Binton also knows that the system has its limits. One, of course, would have been us getting some solid evidence against him for Doyle's killing. We didn't. And he was confident we wouldn't. Another prohibitive limit—and this is where you come in—is for him to be identified by the media.'

Kate was wriggling with comments but he gestured for her to hear him out.

'The Establishment can shut me up, same as they can Taff Roberts. They can bring limited pressure on you lot, may indeed already have done so on your editor. But if

Lawrence Cawley really gets his teeth into a high-level murder cover-up, well, the more D-notices the better so far as he's concerned. And, believe you me, the POA and upwards are all aware of that danger. So, too, is Binton. Okay? You with me now?'

'Yes. And the bone I keep choking on is my benighted editor. Proof: that's what Larry's going to be bleating for.'

'No problem. My bet is that the POA will oblige us with that.'

'But *how?*'

'What we're at here is a game of bluff. We've already got the lines open to the union via your deputy editor; so tomorrow he can stir things up on that front. As for friend Binton, in my view what that cocky bastard needs is what you TV people call a good visual.'

DAY SIX

CHAPTER 15

For cameraman Peter Marse it turned out definitely the season's most bizarre non-assignment. But for the fact that he both liked and secretly fancied Kate Lewis, he'd likely not have got drawn into it in the first place.

She had telephoned him late the previous evening to ask could he possibly bring the lightweight VT gear he kept at home for rush jobs and meet her before eight next morning outside Brentford prison. He should have quizzed her more fully—should then have telephoned in to check with ITN, both for a project number and fuller details. He didn't. After all, it was Kate and it was late and what the hell.

Given the cold drizzle of dawn, however, it had all begun to seem hugely less of a lark—and less so still when Ms Lewis confirmed that indeed there was no project number because indeed she had initiated the assignment entirely on her todd.

'Not working to Larry on it?'

'No, Pete, to the CID.'

'God above, why didn't you *tell* me?'

'You'd have cried off.'

'Damn sure I would. Which is what I'm doing right now!'

'Come on, Pete love, it's only a quickie—a snatch shot of one of the screws as he comes off duty.'

'*Only!*' Marse groaned, fumbling for his cigarettes. 'Anyway, what's your game, working for the Law? I mean, is this Katie Lewis I'm sat with here or is it some snide little copper's nark?'

'ITN'll use it, don't worry. Scoop of the month. Lawrence'll be ecstatic.'

'Then why hasn't he okayed it? Why no project number? I mean, you've got to know you're costing me here, darling. And not just overtime. By luring me out like this, you've put me in breach of contract, outside union regs, the Press Council, you name it.'

'Yes, Pete. Sorry, Pete. You're still the best, Pete.'

He snorted, then lit a cigarette. Kate opened the car window.

'So anyway, where are they—these CID masters of yours?'

'Over there. The red Mini opposite the gates.'

'That's your car.'

'Yes, but the man sitting inside it happens to be the same chief super you filmed here on the evening of the riot—now waiting to signal us when Binton comes out.'

She omitted to add that, being officially off the investigation, Jack Walsh was set on keeping the lowest possible profile, indeed was only at the prison at all because there had been no other way of identifying Binton for them.

The cameraman, although he decided not to leave her to get on with it alone, promptly withdrew into a sulk, smoking in a silence as dour as the weather and leaving Kate to shiver beside the open window.

Prison staff were already arriving for the morning shift, turning into the car park opposite the gates while those with motorbikes or cycles turned in towards the forecourt bike sheds. By eight o'clock the light had improved enough for Kate to distinguish the twin cameos of Elizabeth Fry and John Howard high on the gatehouse towers. And what, she wondered, would the Victorian reformers think now. What indignation to find all those humane single cells now used for threeing-up; as for all those workshops that were now used as little more than day rooms where prisoners exchanged gossip and reinforced each other's criminality . . . !

It took Victorian prosperity and conceit finally to banish the Newgate era but the austerity of twentieth-century cutbacks to end the ideals and reverse the enlightenment. But then, did prison ever really change, other than for the worse? And yet . . . and yet . . . if today's abominations provoked some revisions in sentencing—if the scandal of the penal dustbins at least forced the courts to explore such things as community-service orders and intermediate treatment as alternatives to custody—then there could yet prove some warped virtue in it.

The night-shift staff were beginning to leave now: filling out from the gate-office door, hunching deep into their dark blue anoraks, hurrying across to the bikes or the car park, silent for the most part, their mood dampened by the Saturday morning weather, few blinking more than a half-curious glance at the two occupied cars parked opposite the gates.

Kate was keeping her gaze on Walsh who was straining to glimpse each man's face as he left. Behind her in the back seat, Marse had his TV camera at the ready but held low out of sight.

Time passed, but with no sign of Binton. In fact, when they had checked with Ashley Pelham the previous evening, he had said it was by no means certain Binton would be on duty. Since the man had been working a day shift at the start of the week, he must subsequently have arranged a duty swap with one of the night-shift men. It was likely they'd have swapped for the entire remainder of the week, but it could equally have been for just the one night since that was all Binton needed to fire Hythe's cell.

In the event, for all his surveillance skills, the detective almost missed their man. No car or bike or even service-issue anorak for health freak Binton but trainers and tracksuit, his face partly hidden by the raised weather hood as he left the gate-office door at a fast jog. He vaulted the barrier, came swinging out between the wrought-iron gateposts and headed off left along the pavement. It all happened so swiftly that Walsh had to abandon their planned signal and instead blink the car lights and point along after the already distant jogger. So much for plans.

Kate reversed rapidly into the car park gateway for a two-point turn and, barely avoiding a collision, accelerated off in pursuit.

'Try and pan him as we go past, Pete. Then I'll stop well ahead so you can track him in on the zoom from a long-shot.'

It didn't work. The panning shot was spoilt by oncoming traffic and unevenness of the road surface, while the long-shot track never even got started. Binton must have glimpsed the camera as they first passed him because, by the time Kate had pulled up ahead, the prison officer had swung away down a side track. They turned left to try and intercept his possible route but in vain.

'Useless,' the cameraman growled, stowing his gear and consoling himself that at least the editor knew nothing of it and their failure need go no further. 'So what are you grinning at?'

'I didn't tell you before, Pete old love, but part of the exercise was to let Binton know we're on to him.'

'You what?'

'Apparently it's known in Yard parlance as flushing him.'

'Makes us sound like a blooming toilet!'

'Yes, well, given Binton's character, that's about right.'

'Tanner promised to ring through with the address when he gets to the prison later this morning.' The deputy editor cocked his head, eyeing Kate quizzically. 'Whatever has he done, this bloke Binton? I thought Tanner was about to swallow the phone when I told him the name.'

'An abbreviated military career serving in Ulster, followed by a few years in the service of HM Prisons, culminating in an excess of Mufti zeal on Monday when he disposed of IRA bomber Pat Doyle and then on Friday tried to incinerate Ron Hythe. Nothing unacceptable or likely to lose him any Brownie points just so long as he remained anonymous—which, thanks to us, he no longer is. Hence the question now is less what he's done so much as what he's about to do.'

'Like, come and incinerate ITN?'

'Who knows? Meantime, Steve, old sport, how about trying to chase us up something on Binton's military record?'

'Corporal with the Second Paras.' He grinned, wagging a finger at her. 'Tanner told me that much. I've already booked a call through to an RSM contact of mine at regimental HQ.'

'Such overwhelming efficiency, Steve.'

'More so than you, right now.' Then, at her look: 'You're late for your interview with the mandarin.'

'I understood we were going to talk about the Brentford riot, Mr Grantley.'

'What gave you that idea?'

'It's surely been your number one preoccupation over the last week.'

'Once again, where did you get that idea?'

'I couldn't divulge my source, sir. Isn't it true? Philip

Knowles reporting directly to you and you to the Home Secretary?'

'Your source has a bizarre notion of Whitehall ways, Miss Lewis.'

'If you say so.' Pause. 'What about the murder investigation? Is that similarly taboo?'

Roy Grantley nodded that indeed it was, his glance frosty with disapproval. But for the challenge of it all, he'd have been tempted to send the baggage packing. He believed in keeping the press most firmly in line, likewise women; and this scrappy young madam qualified on both counts. Her next question reinforced his animosity.

'Is that because it's *sub judice* or because it's now been handed over to Special Branch?'

'Has it been?'

'You, after all, would know.'

'One would hope so.'

It had been, he felt, a plausible enough move, given Doyle's background with the IRA and Binton's with the Paras. Moreover, Commander Johnson was a hundred per cent reliable. Nothing quixotic or indiscreet there, by jove, unlike the unpredictable Walsh who, with this press-hen being so clued-up, was evidently persisting even now with his indiscretions.

Secretary of State Savage had proved gratifyingly pragmatic. Just as well the man was still so new to office and, as such, relatively uncommitted on policy. It had been possible for the mandarin to turn these latest developments to his advantage with almost embarrassing ease. As for the union fraternity, they'd been in a high old flap and in consequence ripe for concessions on such as their separatist demands. By then staging a minor pantomime of concern for the Secretary of State—barely hinting that the Opposition had smelt a cover-up and it was necessary to invoke the Special Branch contingency—it had been possible for Grantley both to secure and entrench the *status quo*, keep the

Prison Department firmly within the empire, defuse the psychopath issue and even advance his own K-status into the bargain.

All being well, the stage was even now being set for the final item in his design, albeit along lines which, while typical of those entrusted with its execution, he did consider just a shade risky and theatrical.

'Do you deny the involvement of Special Branch?'

'Yes, Miss Lewis, I do deny it.'

Not that there was more than a minimal threat involved. Indeed, all being well, the drama should be fully played out in good time for her to catch the evening's first main newscast. She might even enjoy what her evident ambition and resourcefulness deserved: a scoop.

'If you're not going to talk about either the riot or the murder investigation, sir, why am I here?'

'You applied for an interview. Since it's agreed policy between me and my colleagues to make ourselves available to the press from time to time, I fitted you in as soon as was convenient. However, since you were late and time is already running short . . .'

'You agreed to meet but not actually to *say* anything, is that it?'

'Not at all. I assumed you might wish to report on the outcome of a couple of policy-review studies recently concluded on the Prison Department.'

Kate stared. What the hell? Yet she knew better than to underestimate Grantley—knew that he was a survivor, destined soon for his gong, adroit at playing the Establishment game; and yet, for all that, not without some noteworthy legislation to his credit.

'Prison Department policy reviews?'

'For instance, whether any revisions are in order vis-à-vis the custody of psychopaths. Also, whether or not the department should be given autonomy rather than continuing under the wing of mother Home Office.'

*

'That's the one—the semi on the corner.'

'There are lights on upstairs.'

'If we park over there, you can cover both front and back doors and also the garage.'

'Very handy, Kate. Lovely.'

They sat for a while, watching the house. Twice they glimpsed someone moving around upstairs. Then, startlingly, the back door was jerked open by Binton. He stepped briefly back inside and emerged again carrying a suitcase and a holdall to hurry the few metres from the back door to the garage. It was only when he was returning that he glimpsed them watching from the car across the street. He stopped, shock-still, to stare at them . . . whereupon Kate, on a sudden impulse, hopped out of the car and ran across towards him. Binton started fast for the house, only to check in the back doorway as she called out:

'ITN News, Mr Binton!' Then, closing with him: 'Can we have an interview?'

He hesitated, face expressionless, before suddenly stepping aside and gesturing her in. Kate turned to beckon Peter Marse across from the car, but Binton waved him curtly back, meanwhile propelling Kate inside.

Oh Christ, she thought, startled by the swiftness of it all, wincing as she heard the back door closed and then locked behind her. For a sudden desperate moment she wanted to dash through the hallway and keep going straight on outside through the front door. Run for it and to hell with heroism and the stupid job! But no, Katie-girl: you've always wanted attention, the limelight; well, now you've got it all plus a multi-million audience. Look, Daddy! Look at me, Daddy! Look, look, look!'

But, oh dear God, what if he started to get violent?

She turned, swinging to face the man as he came after her into the living-room: no knife, no gun, no implication of physical threat: just a potently well-built male with close-cropped hair and an exaggeratedly erect posture. Erect of stance, she thought absurdly, and pinhole of vision.

His face remained for the most part expressionless, almost studiedly so, making for an oddly impersonal manner which she noticed was matched by the furnishings of the room: standard Jap stereo, TV and video, Scandinavian-style suite and fittings, neutral-coloured carpet and drapes; no pictures or ornaments, no junk or disorder.

'Why've you people been dogging me, Miss Lewis?' His voice had a curious flatness, lacking in inflection.

'You know very well.' He made no response, waiting for her to elaborate, almost forcing her to do so. 'You were one of the Mufti squad on Monday. When you and the others reached the top landing, you left the main assault group. You ran to the toilets at the far end where you struck down Ronald Hythe and then killed Patrick Doyle.'

She found that she was swinging her arms about, perhaps unconsciously trying to counter the mesmeric intensity of his· stare. Resist, she told herself; don't let him dominate you. Okay, so he's a killer; that doesn't make him in any way superior. On the contrary, it diminishes him.

'If that's so,' he remarked, pointing at her, 'how come it's you people outside and not the police?'

'You—er—' keep your head now, Katie-girl; bluff it out, for sweet life's sake—'you can be quite sure they're not far away.' She managed a nod, feeling it in detachment, almost as though observing herself from a distance. 'No doubt they're listening in to us right now, waiting to hear what you have to say.'

Briefly Binton's eyes flickered sideways. Then he was straightening up, drawing breath down into his lower lungs, rising up and settling back. A moment of total repose. When at last he started to talk, it was less a confession than a report.

'Two full tours of duty in Northern Ireland, Miss Lewis,

that's what I served with the Paras. Very exacting work, that. Kill or be killed. Very comprehensive training. Sharpen the reflexes, perfect the techniques.' Briefly his right hand jerked up and sideways in gesture of the killer blow. 'Study the enemy, observe his methods, psyche out his thinking. Survival imperative. Very devious race, the Irish. Two full terms on undercover duties requires the highest degree of perfection. Total dedication and concentration, maximum fitness, both physical and mental.'

He paused to eye her, his expression bleak and detached, then gave a brief nod. 'Two tours was enough—that was their ruling. They were wrong. I could have gone on for a third, even a fourth. But that was their decision. No arguments, no appeal: terminate active service. Transfer or resign.' Another pause, a flick of a pulse, before: 'Naturally, trained up for action and covert duties the way I'd been, there was no question of transferring to the Pay Corps or whatever. God, no. Finish. Resign.'

His eyes checked around the neat, impersonal room, head cocked as thought listening, but when the monotone of his voice resumed, the pace was perceptibly quicker. 'A high quota of dodos in the prison service. The odd one or two worthy of respect, but the majority just time-servers.' A nod, two nods, as though in recollection. 'Naturally, it was the Micks I used to watch. After service in Ulster, that comes as a reflex. Watch, listen, observe. And pretty soon I saw that Pat Doyle wasn't the peasant he seemed. No way. Parading as a big, trouble-making bully. But I could see that behind all that, he was working to a calculated pattern. It takes one to know one, you see. I'd had the covert training to clock the likes of Doyle and suss out what he was up to.' Another nod in punctuation. 'Coordinating subversive activities of the IRA inmates, that was his game. Dead sly, extremely devious. But effective, for all that. Played a major role in fomenting the riot he did. If it hadn't been for Doyle and his cronies, the staff would most likely have contained the whole incident.' Another nod. 'I knew it was him. Instigator, coordinator, *agent provocateur*. So of course, come the assault, I was after him. And when we broke through up to the Fours, I found him—happened to reach the recess, in fact, just as he felled Hythe.' Briefly the chop of the killer hand was repeated. 'An execution. Summary justice. Act of duty. Interests of security—enemy of the realm.' Nod. 'Executed. Terminated.'

Certainly, Kate thought, he showed no hint of conscience over it, no indication in his tone of any remorse at the suffering he had inflicted on Hythe. Indeed, there was an element more of elation than regret. Training, she thought: once you school men in murder, you cancel out their taboos; you shift the element of responsibility on to the masters and away from the self-perceived executioners.

'But—' her voice seemed as remote and detached as her movements—'but the witnesses?'

'Connolly and McGuire? No problem. Totally reliable. Totally familiar with the rules for survival inside. "Ron Hythe did it, guv . . . we saw him, guv."'

'They lied to protect you?'

'To protect themselves, Miss Lewis.' He cleared his throat, a short barking sound akin to an expletive. 'And that stupid pratt Hythe—given a grain of sense, he'd have done the same. Self-defence, manslaughter, like his brief kept telling him; nominal sentence absorbed into his Life term. No sweat. But no, he went and broke the rules. Pathetic little poofter, listening to the copper.' He grimaced, gesturing in exasperation. 'A no-no! A convicted wife-killer who'd have been hung for his troubles not so long ago! No, Miss Lewis, Ronald Hythe had to pay for that. Had to.'

'By *burning*?'

'He wouldn't have *known*—not if he'd done it right, how it was planned. Not if he'd smoked the laced-up joint, put himself out proper and slept through it. No sweat.'

'Except—' she had to swallow to retrieve her voice—

'except he survived, after a fashion, and now it's you who've got to pay.'

Briefly the officer's mouth curled at the side, though whether in irony or defiance she was unsure. 'I don't think so, Miss Lewis. Survival training, you see. Total fitness, optimum resources. Qualities of prime value in extremes like this.'

He pointed to a chair, signalling for her to sit. This is it, Kate thought, this is where it gets messy. This is where your notorious daughter hits new peaks of prominence, Daddy.

She never saw the blow coming—merely realized that the blade-like hand had sliced across to skin her ear in a lethal karate chop. The speed and precision of the blow jerked her backwards, head hard against the chairback, muscles rigid with shock. Yet Binton made no move to follow it up, seemingly content with the single demonstration.

'That's the one,' he remarked, straightening up, face expressionless as he allowed the killer hand to chop—flick-flick—like an eye-blink against the open palm of his other hand. '*Tegatana–Ganmen-Uchi.*'

Kate tensed with terror, her eyes fixed on him. Binton studied the edge of his palm a moment, then turned, moving out to the hallway where he paused to give her a formal nod before closing the door. She heard him turn the key in the lock, then hurry quickly off through the kitchen and outside.

Briefly Kate gave way to the reaction churning inside, her hands, her limbs, her whole body trembling uncontrollably. But then, as quickly, the reporter instincts took over: get after it, stay near the action!

Still shaking, she managed to get herself up and across to check the door. Locked, sure enough, as also were the big, inner panes of the window's double-glazing. Right then, lass, get at it! Alarmingly, her first attempt to smash her way out proved ludicrously inept, the chair rebounding ineffectively from the toughened glass panel. In rising desperation, she grabbed the video, wrenching it clear and climbing up on the table so as to heave it with all her strength end-on at the glass. It cracked apart with a noise, like a rifle-shot, the video smashing on to splinter its way through the outer frame.

It was several seconds after Kate had eased her way gingerly through the jagged hole, gasping still with exertion and haste, that the car bomb detonated.

The blast, although it completely demolished the asbestos garage, did little more than fling Kate down, shocked and breathless, at the corner of the house.

Pete Marse was out of his car, camera trained on the devastation as he moved cautiously forward. Midway across to the wrecked garage he paused, focusing down on to something among the debris in the road. Kate, sobbing with shock and reaction, tottered to his side to stare down at the charred object barely recognizable as a severed limb.

'ITN had been shadowing Prison Officer Binton following the receipt of information that he was responsible for the death of convicted IRA bomber Patrick William Doyle during last Sunday's riot at Brentford prison.

'When ITN approached Binton at his home here in Carling Lane, Twickenham, this afternoon, he agreed to talk to me but not in front of the camera. He told me that until three years ago he had served as a corporal in Northern Ireland with the Second Paratroop Regiment, with whom he claimed to have been engaged in undercover activities.

'Whatever those activities involved—and this evening the Minstry of Defence declined to supply any details—it appears that today the IRA caught up with the one-time Paras corporal. For within minutes of the blast at Twickenham, ITN's Dublin office received a call from an IRA spokesman claiming responsibility for the bomb—planted, so it was alleged, in vengeance for the murder of Doyle. And, later this evening an army bomb expert sifting through the wreckage confirmed to me that the blast bore all the

distinctive hallmarks of an IRA detonation. Whether the
IRA are correct in attributing Doyle's murder to Prison
Officer Binton, however, is likely to remain uncertain.

'What is known to ITN is that suddenly yesterday afternoon the two CID officers in charge of the murder investigation at Brentford Prison were recalled to Scotland Yard
and ordered to hand the case over to a senior Special Branch
officer believed to be of commander rank. Whether anything
further will ever be heard of that investigation now that
Angus Binton has met this violent end will have to remain
a matter for speculation.

'Kate Lewis, News at Ten, Twickenham.'

DAY SEVEN

CHAPTER 16

'Kate, old sport, the Yard and the Home Office have both
issued flat denials. They're contradicting your claim that
the case had been handed over to Special Branch.'

'Oh boy!' What a lousy profession! What a lunatic way
to earn a living! Predictable enough, I guess.'

'But none the less embarrassing for ITN.'

'Are they offering to field Foxy Walsh to back their
denials?'

'If needs be, I should think.'

Kate scowled over it a while. Apart from cameraman
Pete Marse seeing the chief outside the prison the previous
morning, she had absolutely no corroboration—other perhaps than Taff, and to heck with that. Whatever Taff's
feelings for her, damn sure her loyalty to him would remain
sacrosanct. Discretion ruled!

'Has it occurred to you,' she asked the editor by way of a
counter-attack, 'how exceedingly convenient that car bomb

was for everyone: no more questions asked, no risk of any embarrassing court hearings or independent inquiries. Just BANG—end of problem.'

'Ironic, I grant you, the IRA doing the Brit Establishment such a big favour.'

'But, Lawrence, *did they*? Can we be entirely sure it was them?'

The editor sighed, eyeing her with distaste. Typical prima donna's response: one brief fling of glory and she became insufferable.

'Look, it was the usual IRA spokesman who made contact —usual procedures, usual codewords, the lot.'

'Brit Intelligence are familiar with those procedures and codewords. They could have set and detonated the bomb, then faked a call from the IRA claiming responsibility.'

'If they had, be sure we'd have had the Dublin gang on to us quick as light the moment you reported it. But we didn't. No comeback.' He shook his head, reaching to light up the day's first cheroot. 'Look, Sister Anna, it's obvious that Connolly and McGuire somehow managed to send Binton's name to Dublin. To hell with telling anything to Walsh and Co; they'd *obviously* prefer their own system of justice. Elemental—and terminal.'

'Hm. And the Special Branch connection?'

'Uncorroborated . . .'

'But fact, goddamn it, Lawrence. Fact! Don't you start denials. Why should Walsh and his DI have been suddenly taken off the case the moment they got too close to the real killer?' Then, persisting: 'And more, why didn't Special Branch pull Binton in once they knew of all the circumstantial evidence linking him via the Mufti to Doyle's death and to the cell fire? Why, Lawrence? It's almost as though they were deliberately holding off so as to let the Irish take him out.'

'Maybe they were, Kate, maybe they were, However, we can be absolutely certain we'll never be able to prove they were even involved, much less holding off.'

'Hm.' Kate stomped across to get her coat. 'We'll see.'

'Where are you off to?'

'The Twickenham coroner's due to open the inquest on Binton. I'll be curious to hear what evidence of identification they offer on the remains—such as they were.'

Broken and mutilated though the corpse had been, the evidence of its identification—as marshalled by the coroner's officer and duly confirmed by sworn testimony from both Binton's sister and the local pathologist—was impressively credible. Binton's Service issue wristwatch, the tattoos on his arms, scars from an appendectomy operation and also a childhood accident, conformity with dental records —all were offered along with supportive photographic evidence, to reinforce the sister's tearful assurance that, although they had been gruesomely damaged by the force of the blast, she was satisfied that the remains of the facial features were indeed those of her late brother. Whereas it was true that she and Angus had been largely estranged since the time of his enlistment in HM Armed Forces, she was none the less sure it was her brother.

Kate was hard put to fault the proceedings—or the coroner's conclusion of a positive identification. Only two aspects offered even a crumb to her suspicions: first, the coroner broke with the open-court tradition by announcing that, because of the violent nature of the death and its obvious terrorist connections, he would be withholding Miss Binton's married name and address for reasons of her personal security. Secondly, when Kate tried to approach and speak to the distressed sister, she found herself warded politely aside by the coroner's officer while the sister was whisked astutely away by a young man who, though he *could* have been her husband, also happened to fit the classic mould of a Special Branch officer.

*

After the inquest, Kate called in at her home on the offchance of a message from Taff. Miraculously, wonderfully, it paid off, the Ansafone pronouncing his plea for reconciliation.

Kate telephoned through to Scotland Yard, asked for Taff's extension and, to her surprise, found herself instead connected through to his sly old guv'nor.

'Yes, Miss Lewis?'

'I was trying to return a call from Taff.'

'Inspector Roberts isn't on duty until later today. His calls are being put through to me.' Predictably enough, she thought, given the denials. 'That was a remarkable scoop you managed to pull off yesterday at Twickenham, Miss Lewis.'

'Wasn't it just, Mr Walsh—all thanks to you.'

Silence. No reply. But did they, she wondered, did they really monitor the calls of such high-ranking officers at the Yard.

'And this morning, also thanks to you, I've been dropped in it over my sweet head.'

'Sorry?'

'Quite possibly I shall be up before the Press Council for irresponsible misreporting of facts. Specifically, my report that the case had been taken away from you and handed over to Special Branch.'

'Ah.' She could imagine that hard, sardonic grin beneath the tufted eyebrows. 'Yes, I can appreciate how that sort of detail is tricky to verify if challenged.'

'Which it has been—both by the Home Office and by your superiors.' Pause. 'No point in my asking you to verify it, I suppose.'

'Given the escalation of events, Miss Lewis, there would indeed seem to be very little point. Given that the case is now closed.'

'To everyone's convenience—except mine.'

'Sorry?'

'The Press Council hearing . . .'

'It won't come to that, Miss Lewis, as you very well know.'

'If it does, I could very well be obliged to call you to give evidence.' Pause. 'You or Detective-Inspector Roberts.'

Pause. Kate let the silence run, waiting for him to hang up. He didn't.

'It's not for me to lecture you on the confidentiality of your contacts, of course, but you might care to reflect on the career damage such a move could mean for young Roberts.'

And okay, Foxy Walsh, so you've got me weighed up, Kate reflected as she rang off and hurried outside to her car; but I'm damned if I'll let you off that particular hook in a hurry. I love him as a man; but to you he's a blessed son. So you can just sweat awhile for your betrayal.

'About your TV celebrity . . .'

'Kate been on to you, has she, guv'nor?'

'She has, yes. Breathing fire and threatening subpœnas.'

'Over?'

'Transfer of the case to Special Branch.'

'Oh aye?' Taff sat down, eyeing his chief, tickled by the irony. 'I rather thought Gaffer Blaize would rise to that one.'

'Him and the Home Office both. Highly sensitive.'

'Well, naturally, guv'nor. Devious skulduggery like that.'

'Oh?' Walsh's expression was cold with latent rebuke. 'Like what?'

'Like tipping off the IRA as to the identity and whereabouts of Doyle's killer.'

The chief snorted in curt rejection. 'You've been reading too much Left-wing pap.'

'If you say so, guv'nor.'

'I do.'

'Fact is, they did take it away from us and give it to the spooks. I find that distinctly disturbing.'

'Listen, lad . . .'

'What about answerability here, guv'nor? What about democratic control of the forces of law and order?'

'What about them?'

'I'd like to know just who our masters are here.'

'Masters?'

'Okay, I work to you; you work to Mr Blaize. Chain-of-command, tunnel-vision stuff. Ask not, just obey. Great! But, just for once, you and me have had a peep up the line. The orders are coming from the wrong place and for the wrong reasons. You may be near enough to that fat retirement job for you to be able to swallow it, *sir*, but it sure as hell chokes me.'

They met in classic cloak-and-dagger style beside the lake in St James's Park, both tossing snacks to the listless waterfowl. Harold, being primarily the MoD's Deep Throat to ITN's military correspondent, was curious to meet Kate—the more so since her spectacular presence at the Twickenham bomb jobbie the previous day.

'In point of fact, there's not a great deal to add on Corporal Binton over and above what you reported last night, Miss Lewis. Two tours of duty in the Paras; some covert ops but all low-level and routine.'

The latter rather seemed to sum up Harold himself, Kate decided: studiously grey and unremarkable.

'What about his forced resignation?' she asked. 'Surely there had to be something sinister behind that.'

'Depends on your definition. If you consider it sinister that a young man's military training and experience of active service in Ulster can result in a medical report classifying him as a *dangerous liability*, then yes, I agree that could be seen as sinister.'

'Classified, in effect, as a potential killer.' Kate was aware of the irony, given the job spec for a soldier.

'Ah, but inclined to spontaneous impulses and wanting in moral constraints.'

'So, for medical read psychological, yes?'

'Yes, indeed.' Harold finished his first packet of duck pellets and opened a second. And highly probable, Kate decided, that he was similarly tossing her prepackaged scraps of information, cleared in advance with his superior, just to keep her quiet.

'One could equally argue that his identification as high risk by the medics demonstrates the exercise of responsible precautions.'

'Except that they resulted in his being let lose on society —albeit a criminal one—where the killer impulse ultimately led to fatal results.'

'Yes.' Harold seemed genuinely wistful about it. 'Ironically, being medical, that report was confidential and was hence not available *per se* to the Home Office personnel who processed Binton's application to join the prison service.'

'One final question: the IRA took the credit, gladly enough, I'm sure, but just who was it actually set the bomb?'

'That's something we'll never know, Kathy-love. Never.'

'Don't you find that sinister?'

'Yes.'

'Yet you're still content to serve them as masters and play along with their system?'

'No.' Taff grimaced, stung by the reproach, uneasy still over the compromise with which he had earlier had to wrestle and come to terms. 'Not content with it. But not sufficient of a rebel to stand up and be counted.'

He paused, easing back on the accelerator as he glanced sidelong at her. 'How about you?'

'Me?' Kate shrugged, echoing his own phrase back at him. 'Absolutely, yes—and double pay on Sundays.'

'In which case, Kathy-girl, suppose we celebrate that by getting married?'

'*Ha!*'

He let some time go by, filtering them off the trunk road,

hoping she'd keep her mind on their destiny rather than their destination.

'Agreed,' he resumed, 'what we're looking at here is one of the uglier warts on the face of democracy. But then, as the man said, democracy is the worst system except for all those other systems which have been tried and failed. So, on that basis, I'm prepared to compromise—to go along with it and dance to their tune.' Then, glancing at her in appeal: 'Water finds its own level. Okay, lover, so now you know my level. If that's genuinely below yours, fair enough, we'll forget it and go our separate ways.'

Or else start life together on the strength of a mutual compromise, Kate reflected ruefully. So much for integrity and honour!

'Is it Kate you're asking or only Kathy?'

'It's Kathy I love.' Then, with a wry snort: 'However on the basis that one compromise begets another, I'm prepared to settle for Kate.'

'Typically sly Lloyd George answer that is!' Then, persisting over his reply: 'You realize if I take you on—flawed, compromised professional copper that you are—we shall spend the rest of our natural together squabbling over this or similar issues, reliving the Binton case in one form or another, savaging and tearing at each other, only to replenish each new day from the depths of our Promethean obstinacy . . .'

'And love . . .'

'Shut up, you don't know what I'm talking about. You haven't been married before. I have.'

'Not to me.'

'Dear God, the conceit of the man!'

They were driving through the Pinner sprawl, she noticed, wondering vaguely where he was taking her.

'Anyway,' he resumed, 'whoever set the bomb, I'm sure my sly old guv'nor was right about there being no initial cover-up. Nothing coordinated, at least; no one masterminding an overall plan. Simply that each separate limb of the Establishment octopus—the prison's admin staff, the officers' union, the Civil Service mandarins, the politicians —each was resorting spontaneously to the same survival reflex.'

'Ha. Before finally flushing the last indigestible lump down the IRA sewer!' Kate grimaced and then turned, gesturing impatiently at the way ahead. 'Come on then, drop the mystery. Where are you taking me?'

The DI pulled a face, embarrassed at involving her like this. But, hang it, if she was such a committed professional, she should know how to cope with life, and flesh, in the raw. 'To Northwood,' he mumbled. 'Mount Vernon hospital, to be exact. There's someone there who needs a visit. One of the Forgotten People.'